Not Just
Proms & Parties

Emily's Rebellion

Not Just Proms & Parties: Emily's Rebellion
Text © 2008 Patricia G. Penny

Published by Lobster Press™
1620 Sherbrooke Street West, Suites C & D
Montréal, Québec H3H 1C9
Tel. (514) 904-1100 • Fax (514) 904-1101 • www.lobsterpress.com

Publisher: Alison Fripp
Editors: Meghan Nolan & Faye Smailes
Editorial Assistant: Lindsay Cornish
Graphic Design & Production: Tammy Desnoyers

Library and Archives Canada Cataloguing in Publication

Penny, Patricia G., 1953-
     Emily's rebellion / Patricia G. Penny.

(Not just proms & parties)
ISBN-13: 978-1-897073-73-5

     I. Title. II. Series: Penny, Patricia G., 1953- . Not just proms
& parties.

PS8631.E573E54 2008   C813'.6   C2007-904855-2

Printed and bound in Canada.

To my husband, Bob, who makes the sun shine for me.

– Patricia G. Penny

Not Just Proms & Parties

Emily's Rebellion

written by
Patricia G. Penny

Lobster Press™

Chapter 1

My mother is at it again. She's unloading the dishwasher and throwing the knives and forks into the drawer as though *I'm* in there.

"I don't see why you have to be so mad about it. It's not *your* body." I cross my arms and lean back against the kitchen counter. I know it's the wrong thing to say, but sometimes stuff just falls out of my mouth before my brain has had a chance to think it over. Spinning toward me, she gives me that look, the one that says she is totally losing it.

"*Your body*, Emily, is only fifteen years old! A tattoo done by a – did you call him an *artist*? – is stupid! Look at you –" Her eyes fill with tears as she pulls back the strap of my tank top and looks again at the winged dragon etched just above my left breast – "with a goddamned dragon, of all things!"

"I like it." I twist my shoulder away and go over to sit at the table.

"Tell me that when you're fifty. Or even thirty. In fact, I bet you'll be sorry by this time next year," she says before pausing. "I'm making an appointment for you to have blood work done to make sure you didn't contract any diseases from this *artist*'s tools!" She slams the drawer shut, just as I knew she would. "A dragon! Wait till your father sees it."

"He already knows about it."

"He *knows*?" She has turned to look at me again, hands on her hips, eyes narrowed. I'm glad our kitchen has an island. It keeps some space between us.

"I told him when I was at his place last weekend. He said he wasn't going to tell you. He figured you'd freak out about it." Dad bought a condo a few blocks from the house when he and Mom split a few months ago. My brother Frankie and I drop in on him whenever we like. I'm wondering if maybe I should head over there right now.

Mom and I stare at each other for a minute

while she probably tries to figure out how she will deal with me *and* Dad. Finally she just throws her hands up and walks out of the room. I can hear her in the front hallway, grabbing her keys off the hall table and pulling the door open. She tries to slam the door behind her, but it just sucks closed with a sad, muffled thump. I smile with satisfaction. I can hear her car start and I know she'll pull out of the driveway too fast and tear off down our quiet street like a NASCAR driver. Good luck to anyone who gets in her way.

I go upstairs and flop onto my bed with my feet hanging over the edge. I'm tall, taller than any of the girls I hang out with, and my friend Maddy tells me that I could be on magazine covers. I have "the look," she says. Hazel eyes, dark hair, olive skin. I used to believe her, but I know now that I don't have the pouty lips or the boney shoulders that it takes to be in the business. I'm thinking about tearing down the pictures of models that have covered my bedroom ceiling since I was a kid. I'm not into high fashion anymore. I'm more into tight jeans that are low enough to make my mother cringe.

On the wall across from me is one of those huge inspirational posters of chubby angels. Frankie went at it with a black Magic Marker a couple of years ago, so now they are devil-angels with barbed tails and pointed horns. Frankie must have known I had it in me even then, back when things were good around here.

I take a deep breath, reach for my cell phone, punch the speed dial and wait, half expecting to reach a voice message. After a few rings, I hear my grandmother pick up at the other end. I sigh loudly into the phone. "Hi, Grams."

"Emily? What's wrong? You sound like the world is coming to an end." She's right. Even I can tell that I'm over-dramatizing.

"Oh, nothing. Mom and I just had another fight." I can hear traffic in the background of wherever Grams is. "She's always treating me like a child."

"Oh, Emily. I wish you two would get along better. You're like a couple of hamsters in the same cage. I worry that one of you is going to end up flushed down the toilet." Grams is hilarious. That's why I like calling her. "So what's the problem now? Did you spend too much on new clothes? Bring home a C on your math test? Rob a bank?"

"Yeah, Grams – I robbed a bank. Mom wouldn't have minded except that it was *her* bank. She told me to hit yours next time."

"You'd be disappointed," she says dryly. Not likely. I'm pretty sure that Grams has plenty of money.

"She's mad because I got a tattoo," I admit.

"A tattoo?" She laughs, which is what I wish my mom could have done when I told her. "What is it? A butterfly on your ankle?"

"A dragon on my boob."

"Oh, charming!" she laughs again. "Maybe I'll get one of those."

"Yuck! That's just scary," I inform her. "On me, it's more … artsy."

"Well, you've always been the artistic one in the family," she agrees. I hear her car engine shut off. "I'm just heading into the gym," she tells me. "Got to get into shape for my trip to Italy. Why don't you come and join me? You used to love working out with me."

"No thanks. I'll just hang here. Watch some TV."

"Boring! You're still going to be watering my plants while I'm away, right?"

"Yep – twice a week, no over-watering."

"Ten dollars for every plant that's still alive when I get home. How does that sound?"

"Okay, but they all have to be healthy before you leave."

"Deal. You're coming by after school tomorrow to pick up the keys?"

"Yep." Grams lives in a condo right across from school. Sometimes Maddy and I go there for lunch and watch soaps with her.

"And think about making up with your mother, okay? She's only upset because you let someone use your perfectly good body as a canvas. And if I'm not mistaken, you're underage. Hmm?"

"Yeah, but –"

"Yeah, but! Make up with your mother before she runs someone over at an intersection."

"Too late. She's out there on the road already."

"Thank God I'm parked!" She hesitates for a second. "You know you're going to have to try harder to get along with her, Em. She's going through a bad time and she's just … edgy. You're not making it any easier for her by defying her like that right now. Can't you put that whole teen rebellion thing off for a year or so? Give her a chance to get over your dad and be herself again?"

"I'm not *trying* to be a pain. This is just who I am."

"Don't be so sure. You and your mother are very much alike."

"Oh, like I want to hear that!"

"Take it as a compliment. Your mother is fabulous and you know it. She's just trying to find herself. And so are you."

"Have you been reading *O Magazine* again, Grams?"

"There's some good advice in there!" she laughs. "Go on. Kiss and make up."

"I guess." My voice is flat.

"Love you, Em."

"You too." I flip my phone shut and sigh. She's right. My mother and I used to be really close until she and my father separated. I don't know why we can't seem to get along anymore. All I know is that she's unhappy all the time and never has any patience with me. But one thing is for sure: I'm not going to apologize for who I am. If she doesn't like me, it's her problem. *She's* the one who kicked Dad out. *She's* the one who ruined everything.

I hear the sound of a car turning into the driveway. I roll over on the bed and pull the blinds back from the window. Crap! My mother is back already.

I decide not to go downstairs. If she wants to come and apologize to me, she knows where I am. Why should I have to be the one who says sorry?

I rub my fingers absently over my new tattoo and think about the two months that Grams will be gone. Her condo will be empty that entire time and I'll have her keys. It will be like having my own place, somewhere to escape the constant criticism of my mother. I can feel my mood improving already. Once I have those keys, I'll be able to do whatever what I want.

Chapter 2

My mother comes into the kitchen while I'm making toast the next morning. She smiles and tries to act as though we never even had an argument last night. I guess it's her way of apologizing.

"I'll be late tonight, so just heat up the leftover lasagna," she tells me while she's pouring herself a coffee. "I've got a class from seven to ten."

"Do you want me to do anything, like laundry or something?" She has to know that this is as close as I'll get to telling her that I'm willing to meet halfway. I'd never offer to do laundry otherwise.

"That would be nice of you." It's like a dance

and we're both trying not to step on each other's feet. She picks up her laptop and her coffee and glances around the room as if she's looking for something.

"They're over by the back door," I tell her, and she goes over to pick up her keys.

"See you later," she tells me sort of sadly, and she hesitates long enough that I finally go over and give her a quick hug. She doesn't hug me back, but her hands are full and she'd probably spill her coffee. When she leaves I feel sort of empty, as if I've let her down again. I hate it when she makes me feel guilty.

Frankie comes bounding down the stairs and into the kitchen. He's only two years older, but we really don't have a lot of common interests, although we laugh at the same stuff. I guess we have a sort of bond, having shared the same experience of watching our parents give up on whatever had held their marriage together for twenty-two years.

"Where's Mom?" he demands, looking around the room as if I've hidden her someplace.

"She left for work."

"Oh man! I wanted some money."

"What for?"

"School trip. We're going to the Baseball Hall

of Fame."

I snort. "Like she'd give you money for that! Dad just took us there six months ago. Besides, it isn't educational."

"*Educational?*" he asks. "You mean like your class shopping trip to New York?"

"We went to the museum and the library," I remind him.

"No, *the class* went to the museum and the library," he says. "You and Maddy snuck off and went to Fifth Ave for the afternoon."

"I wish I'd never told you," I mutter.

"I need sixty bucks for a school parking pass, too."

"Well don't look at me," I say haughtily. "You're the one with the job! It's not like *I* work at the gas station."

"I don't get paid until the fifteenth."

"So walk like the rest of us."

He grabs a banana from the counter and heads down the hall, complaining. I pick up my schoolbag and go out the back door. "I'm gone!" I yell back into the house before closing the door.

Maddy is waiting for me at the corner already. Even though she is much shorter than me, the teal T-shirt I loaned her last week fits her perfectly and the color looks great with her blond hair.

She sees me from about half a block away and waves giddily before bouncing toward me. "Guess what?"

"You won tickets to the concert!" Her birthday is coming up soon and she is hoping to spend it front-row center at some upcoming rock concert she's been dying to see.

"No, I met a guy." Maddy has been on the rebound after a recent breakup. I guess finding a new boyfriend must be as important to her as winning those tickets.

"Oh yeah? Who?" A little part of me is jealous. My own life definitely has room for a relationship, but I haven't had a boyfriend since Dario Encasca and I hung out in the eighth grade. That doesn't even count.

She turns and walks with me past the big homes on my tree-lined street. "His name is Jeremy something. I met him last night when Tobi and I were at the mall."

"Is he cute?"

She hesitates. "Not so much cute. He's … different. Kind of *dangerous* looking." We cross at the corner without checking for traffic.

"Dangerous how? Does he have piercings?" I ask optimistically. I've been thinking about getting my navel pierced."

"I don't think he has piercings. Nothing I could see, anyway," she answers. It's just as well. Maddy is a whole wheat bread and low-fat milk kind of girl. She wouldn't go for someone who was too freaky. She doesn't even like my tattoo.

"How old is he?" I ask bluntly. We have always agreed that guys our own age are too immature to even consider as boyfriend material.

"Seventeen. Tobi and I are going to meet him downtown after school today." She grabs my arm excitedly. "Why don't you come too? I need a second opinion anyway – Tobi says he's bad news."

"Why? What's wrong with him?"

She shakes her head. "Nothing. Well, he has long hair." She makes a face. "But Tobi says that she's seen him before and that he's always hanging out with a bunch of guys at the pool hall and at the convenience store on Welbourne."

"And you're going to see him again?" I ask doubtfully. He's a dangerous-looking pool hall guy and you're ... you."

"I think he likes me."

"But you hate long hair," I remind her.

"I didn't say I was going out with him. I'm just meeting him downtown."

"Meeting who?" I hear from behind me. We turn to see that Frankie has caught up with us and is smirking at Maddy.

"Some guy." Maddy looks away and I can see her face is flushed behind her hair. Maddy has a crush on Frankie. Always has. He fits her *real* boyfriend profile perfectly. Clean cut. Athletic. Wears designer labels. Someone her parents would like.

Frankie walks on ahead. We watch as he joins a couple of girls walking a short way in front of us. Maddy looks disappointed.

"Okay, I'll go to see what Tobi's so worried about," I tell her. "But we have to stop at Grams' place first to pick up a set of keys. She's leaving for Italy soon."

***

After school, we go to Grams' condo and she gives me the keys, twenty bucks, and what she considers a quick run-down on how to take care of the plants.

"Your grandmother has so much stuff! It's like a museum in there," Tobi says as we settle into the back of the bus on our way to meet Jeremy. She pulls out a mirror to check her hair, even though her super-short style always looks the same. "I thought we were *never* going to get away."

"But I've got the keys now!" I say gleefully, waving them in front of the others before tucking them into the pocket of my jeans.

"I can't believe we had to run to catch the bus just so Maddy won't be late to meet that guy." Tobi lowers her voice and leans toward me. "He's a friend of B.B. Lawrence's. You know, the *drug dealer*." She wrinkles her freckled nose to tell me what she thinks of *him*, and I just say "Oh," because I don't want to admit that I've never heard of B.B. Lawrence.

Maddy smacks Tobi's arm and frowns. "You don't know that for a fact. You don't even know B.B. Lawrence, do you?"

"Well, duh! Why would I want to know someone like that? He's bad news. And so is this Jeremy guy."

"Whatever. It's not like I'm marrying him," Maddy points out. "I can't even remember his last name."

"It's Mathews," Tobi says, tossing her mirror into her schoolbag and leaning back with her arms folded. "And the only reason I agreed to come with you today was to keep you out of trouble."

"Gee, thanks, Mom!" Maddy laughs.

I decide to change the subject by complaining about school. That keeps us busy until our bus pulls into the main terminal and everyone gets up to leave.

"There he is!" Maddy points out eagerly, her finger pressing on the glass. I lean forward and peer past her through the dry dust on the window.

He is standing by himself, pacing slowly. He's of average height, maybe an inch or so shorter than I am, and he's not so much skinny as slight, his shoulder blades prominent through his white T-shirt, his jeans loose on his narrow hips. His hair is longish, a bit disheveled. He's nothing special, I decide, but then my eyes are drawn to his bare arms and I feel myself suddenly go numb for a second. His arms are wiry, toned, tight. I doubt he's the kind of guy who works out in a gym, but he definitely has firm biceps and for some reason, they are making my breath catch.

He turns and sees Maddy, who is now standing in the aisle, and he nods without smiling. I notice a small scar over his eyebrow. He isn't Maddy's type at all. He's *my* type.

Chapter 3

Tobi and I follow Maddy from the bus and then stand like backup singers behind the headliner. Maddy skips toward him enthusiastically, and he glances over her shoulder as she chatters about the bus ride and whether or not we are late.

"You remember Tobi?" she asks him, pulling Tobi up beside her. "And this is my friend Emily. She wanted to meet you."

He glances up at me and I feel like a dork for being introduced as someone who came all the way downtown just to get a look at him.

"Hey," I say to him.

"Hi." He is looking at me curiously. "Do I know you?"

His eyes are *so* blue. "I don't think so."

He thinks for a moment and then shrugs. "You look familiar."

Maddy happily throws in some details. "Em and I have been in the same class since fifth grade. We've been friends for years. And we met Tobi last year when she moved from Syracuse."

He doesn't seem to care where Tobi used to live. "You look older than Maddy," he says to me, and I blush a little and glance down at his arms again. Wow, I would love to reach out and just touch one.

Maddy gives me a funny look and I get even redder. I hope she doesn't know what I'm thinking. She tells Jeremy that we should all go for pizza, then grabs his arm and turns him away, so that Tobi and I end up following them down the street.

I can't help watching every step he takes. Even though he has slouchy jeans and his hair could use some work, I still think he's really hot. I watch those arms swinging while he walks, and without even having to think about it, I know that it doesn't much matter to me whether Maddy already likes this guy or whether Tobi is right about him being bad news. I'm hooked on him.

We reach an intersection and the "Do Not Walk" sign starts flashing. Jeremy stops Maddy from stepping into the street. As I come up on the other side of him, he brushes against my arm with his own, or maybe I brush him. I'm pretty sure that it's just an accident, but when he turns and looks at me, he doesn't smile. He just looks at me *intently* and I realize that our touching may have been deliberate. Maddy is watching me, and her eyes are narrowed, so I know she thinks so too.

Maddy only met Jeremy yesterday, so he isn't her boyfriend – yet. We've always said that neither one of us would ever steal away a boyfriend from the other, but then *I've* never had a boyfriend for Maddy to want to steal away. And, I argue to myself, she already knows that this guy is not her type. I'd be doing her a favor, protecting her from someone she probably wouldn't even speak to if she wasn't rebounding from her last boyfriend. Besides, she can't be too hung up on him anyway. She said herself that it's not as if they're getting married or anything.

So it's obvious. Jeremy is up for grabs. All I need to do is capture his attention without hurting Maddy's feelings and jeopardizing our friendship. I'll just need to be subtle.

Trouble is, subtlety is not my thing.

★★★

I must have done a pretty bad job of hiding my interest in Jeremy, because by the time we've left him and gotten on the bus to go home, Maddy is furious with me.

"I didn't do anything!" I insist to Maddy for the fifth time. "It just kind of happened."

"It wouldn't have 'just kind of happened' if you hadn't been throwing yourself at him all afternoon." Maddy is stuck between me and the window, her arms crossed defensively and her jaw sticking out so far that I could hang a jacket on it. Someone rings the buzzer, and the bus pulls over to the curb with a jerk, making us bounce forward so that I have to put my hand out to keep from hitting the seat in front of me.

"All I did was talk to him. Besides, *you* asked me to come."

"I asked Tobi to come too, but you didn't see *her* gushing all over him. 'What kind of pizza do *you* like, Jeremy? Where do *you* go to school, Jeremy? Tell me *all* about yourself, Jeremy.'"

"He didn't say very much," I grumble, as though that will somehow make things right.

"And then when you took his *phone number* from him …" She shook her head with disbelief.

"I didn't ask for it! He just wrote it on that napkin and gave it to me!"

She's furious, so there's no point in even trying to talk to her about it. I just sit back and let her fume while the bus jerks its way down the road in the evening traffic. I wish Tobi were on our bus so that there would be someone else to help lighten up the air in here. The driver is probably grateful to be protected by his Plexiglas shielding in case Maddy explodes.

Jeremy liked me. I couldn't help it if he picked up some sort of vibe from me. I couldn't help it if he spent the whole time with his eyes locked on mine. He was so … intense. Not at all Maddy's type. She'll see that in time. Still, he shouldn't have been so obvious about his interest in me. He had practically ignored her while he stared at me. Natalie Portman – that's who he said I looked like. It's a stretch, but it still felt good to hear it.

We are approaching our stop so Maddy stands, waiting for me to get out of her way so that she can step into the aisle. I pull myself to my feet and the two of us wait at the rear doors until the bus draws up to the curb. We step down in silence and she starts walking away from me without saying anything.

"Bye!" I call after her hopefully. She doesn't turn around.

Chapter 4

When I get home, Frankie is in the kitchen with his head in the fridge. "Where have *you* been?" he asks, as though he's somehow responsible for me.

"I got pizza with Maddy and Tobi," I answer, kicking my shoes off at the back door.

"Just as well. There's nothing good to eat here anyway."

"There's lasagna. Mom said we should heat it up."

"It's frozen. I'm going to have some ravioli." He takes a can from the cupboard and bangs around, opening the can, dumping the glob of tomato paste and pasta into a bowl, and then shoves it into the center of the microwave.

I watch him quietly, trying to decide if I

should talk to him about my afternoon. I finally give in and ask. "Do you know Jeremy Mathews?"

He thinks for a second and then snorts. "That loser? He used to play baseball against me when we were kids, remember? He was the pitcher for the Raiders."

That must be why Jeremy had remembered me. I used to go watch Frankie's games when I was younger.

"What makes you say he's a loser?" I ask nonchalantly, brushing crumbs off the table from this morning's breakfast.

"He quit about three years ago. Started hanging out with those guys in the north end. Wes Johnson, B.B. Lawrence, Owen Mitchell ..." The microwave timer goes off. He takes the bowl out, then turns to me suspiciously. "That's not the guy that Maddy was talking about seeing, is it? She'd be in way over her head with that guy."

"I'm pretty sure she won't be seeing him again. Besides, what's it to you?" He doesn't answer, which is just as well. I'm glad when Frankie takes his supper into his room so he can eat in front of the computer like a geek. I wasn't looking for a big discussion about Jeremy anyway. Still, the fact that Frankie doesn't approve of him makes me all the more certain that I want to see him again. No one gets to choose who I hang out with, especially my know-it-all brother.

✶✶✶

The next morning, I come down to the kitchen to find an empty laundry basket sitting on the kitchen table with a note taped to it.

"YOU FORGOT TO DO THE LAUNDRY! IT'S IN THE DRYER. PLEASE FOLD AND PUT AWAY. MOM."

I grab the basket and shuffle over to the laundry room reluctantly. I hate folding. As I take a pair of warm jeans from the dryer and smooth the creases out, my mind goes back to Jeremy. I really don't have a good sense of who he is, but I do know one thing: my mother wouldn't like him. I check the time and decide to leave the towels and sweatshirts in a heap on the dryer. I can do them later.

On my way out of the house, I grab my phone and dial Jeremy's number. I'm already down the driveway before he answers. "Hi," I say, surprised by the slight wobble in my voice. "It's Emily. Um, Maddy's friend."

"Oh, hi." His voice is husky, as though he has just woken up. "What time is it?"

"Almost eight. Sorry – is it too early?"

"No, I guess I should be up anyway."

"I just thought I'd call. Maybe see what you're doing later."

"I've got detention after school. Too many late slips."

"Oh. I'm in trouble too – with my mom. And she was already pissed that I got a tattoo."

"Oh yeah? Where?"

I pause for a second before answering in a suggestively low voice. "I'll have to show you sometime."

"Well, I'll be sure to remind you."

I smile at that and shift my phone to the other ear as I walk. "Anyway, she was already mad and now she's left me a snarky note telling me to do laundry or else. I'm like a servant."

"Do they feed you?" he asks, and I smile at his attempt at humor. I've already figured out that Jeremy is not really comfortable with people, so his little joke feels like a small victory for me.

"Not much. That's why I scarfed down so much of that greasy pizza yesterday. They hadn't fed me for weeks."

"Sounds like my house."

We talk awhile longer and I'm a little nervous, so I ramble on about my art classes, my friends, and anything else that pops into my head. He doesn't say much, but he seems like a good listener.

Finally he says, "I've been thinking – maybe I won't go to detention today."

"Oh. So, do you want to do something after school then?" I ask hopefully.

"I guess. Like what?"

My mind races. It would be best to keep Maddy from knowing I'm seeing him. "How about meeting at Glenborough Park? It isn't far from my school."

"Okay. Three thirty?"

"Three forty-five. It'll give me time to get there." I glance up and see Maddy walking toward the corner from her street. She has seen me on the phone. I wave to her, but her face hardens as she turns to march ahead of me quickly. "I have to go," I say to Jeremy. "See you later."

I flip my phone shut and follow her up the street. She's practically running to make sure that it's impossible for me to catch up, so eventually I quit trying.

The morning passes uncomfortably. Maddy and I are in a couple of classes together and even though I'm trying to act as if everything is normal, she's pretending that I don't exist. We sit right across the aisle from each other in math and we usually whisper through half the class, but now she just stares straight ahead as though she's really into algebra.

At lunchtime, I'm not surprised that Maddy isn't anywhere to be seen in the cafeteria. I find an empty table and eat by myself. I'm already into my dessert when Tobi comes storming over to my table and pulls out a chair across from me.

"You're not really seeing Jeremy later, are you?" she demands. I look at her with surprise. "Maddy told me."

"How does she know?"

"He gave you his number right in front of us yesterday. And she could hear you on the phone this morning."

"I could have been talking to anyone!" I object.

"You shouldn't be seeing him, Em," she tries to convince me. "You're really hurting her feelings. And besides, he's such a loser."

"He is not," I scoff. "You're so wrong about him."

"He hangs out on street corners."

"Is there a law against that? Stop worrying," I laugh. "First you were all over Maddy about seeing him, and now me. We're both good judges of character."

"I guess *I'm* not," she says disappointedly and gets up from her chair. It scrapes loudly across the floor. "I thought you were a better person than this."

"Oh, come on, Tobi! Maddy wasn't even dating him yet." Tobi walks away self-righteously.

The afternoon is no better than the morning. By the end of my last class I'm dying to meet Jeremy in the park. I do some last-minute touch-ups on my makeup and then hurry from the school.

As I step outside, I am stunned to see that Jeremy is standing on the sidewalk. Midway between us, Maddy and Tobi are headed down the stairs. I watch helplessly as the inevitable happens and Maddy notices him. She trots the rest of the way down the stairs, takes a sharp right, and heads quickly toward the buses. Tobi scurries alongside her, talking to her earnestly. I've never seen Maddy walk as fast as she has today. She's charging past everyone, along the row of school buses parked bumper-to-bumper down the street. Tobi looks over her shoulder at me and scowls. I hate that I've hurt Maddy, but it seems as if she and Tobi really want to make this into a huge deal. Whatever. I go down the last few steps to meet Jeremy.

Jeremy is watching in confusion. "What's with them?" he asks.

"Nothing. Don't worry about it." And that seems to be enough for him.

We don't do much, just wander around and sit in the park for a while, but he's so different from anyone else I know that even doing nothing is a turn on. I don't want it to end. I think of the keys for Grams' condo and realize that they are still in my other jeans at home.

"Do you want to come over to my grandmother's place? There's no one home."

He looks at me teasingly. "Are you going to show me that tattoo you were talking about?"

"Maybe! Come on, we'll have to pick up the keys from my house first."

My mother will be home from work in about half an hour, so we should have just enough time to grab them. As we start walking, Jeremy's arm slips behind me and his hand slides down to rest on the curve of my hip. That slows us down some, but I'm not complaining.

Jeremy hesitates slightly when we reach my house. As we head up the double driveway and around the back of the house, I can see that he is staring at our garden and our pool. We go in the back door, which enters into the kitchen, and he looks around the room silently. I notice the open laundry room and the towels on top of the dryer where I had left them. "I'll be hearing about that," I sigh, nodding at the mess. "My mother freaks about the smallest stuff." He smiles and seems to relax a little bit. "I'll be right back. I just have to run upstairs for the keys."

When I come back down, Jeremy is standing in the laundry room, whistling as he folds one of the towels. "I thought I could save you some grief," he says, placing the folded towel in the laundry basket and coming back into the kitchen.

"That is so sweet!" I say, crossing the room to show him how appreciative I am.

We're in the middle of a long kiss when the door opens and my mother walks in.

Chapter 5

"Oh. Am I interrupting?" My mother is standing in the open doorway, surprised to see Jeremy and me locked together.

"Mom, this is Jeremy." Jeremy steps away from me awkwardly. My mother puts down her briefcase and a bag of groceries, closes the door, and slips off her shoes. Her face is composed and calm, but I know she's seething on the inside. This past year has added some lines to her face, especially between her eyebrows. Stuff like this just makes the lines deeper.

"Jeremy? Hello. Nice to meet you."

"You too," he answers, and he steps forward as though he is thinking of shaking her hand, but doesn't.

"Do you go to school with Emily?" she asks. I can see she is trying to assess his age and his background, sort of as if she's conducting a job interview. I can see him through her eyes and I know he isn't meeting her standards.

"No. I live closer to Central High."

"Oh? How did you two happen to meet?" She is smiling, but I can see that it's one of those stiff, polite smiles.

"Maddy introduced us," I answer quickly.

"Oh? You're a friend of Maddy's?" she asks, looking past me to Jeremy.

"I guess. Kind of."

I can see her processing what "kind of" means in the context of friendship. "Would you two like a snack? I just bought some tortilla chips if you want nachos."

"Okay," Jeremy answers. "Thanks."

"Maybe you can go out to the car and get the rest of the groceries for me, Jeremy."

"Yeah, sure." He eases past her, as though trying not to startle her. Opening the door, he looks back and gives me just a hint of a reassuring smile. He must know that I'm in for it. When he's gone, she crosses her arms and looks at me with disappointment.

I start to unpack the bag she has already

brought in. It saves me from looking at her.

"Why haven't I heard of Jeremy before?" she asks lightly.

I shrug. "I've only known him for a little while. We're just friends."

She raises her eyebrows. "Really?"

I shrug again and take the chips from the bag. "Is there salsa?"

"In the fridge." She purses her lips. "Emily?"

"Uh huh?" I open the fridge and dig through the jars on the top shelf.

"No boys in the house when I'm not home, please."

"I didn't know you weren't home until we got here," I say evenly.

"I'm just telling you for next time," she answers, and I can tell she is trying to control her voice because Jeremy is on his way back in. I nod and finish making the nachos.

Mom makes a big show out of putting away the rest of the groceries. With a noisy sigh, she folds the last bit of laundry and parades through the kitchen with the full basket to make her point. She is clearly weirding Jeremy out. We eat our nachos in the kitchen in silence and then he says he has to go.

Mom stands with me at the door when we

are saying goodbye, as though we can't be trusted on our own. I'm furious with her, but I can tell by the look on her face that I'd better not challenge her right now. When Jeremy is gone, she tells me to put the dirty dishes into the dishwasher and wipe off the table.

As I take out the recycling for her, Frankie comes home and reminds us that Dad is taking him to his baseball game tonight. Dad wants to spend every possible minute with us lately, including travel time, so Frankie hardly ever gets to drive to games on his own anymore. He's complaining that he's the only guy on his team who still has a parent at his practices when Dad shows up, twenty minutes early. He doesn't bother to knock at the back door. He just comes in as though he still lives here.

"Emily had a boy over after school," my mother says to him before he has a chance to say hello.

"Who?" Frankie demands, as though she is talking to him. I scowl.

"Jeremy Mathews," I tell my father, as though he is the one who asked for a name.

"A new boyfriend?" my dad asks.

"There haven't been any old boyfriends, Dad."

Frankie just won't let it go. "Jeremy Mathews? I thought you said he was interested in Maddy."

"No, I said Maddy met him after school one day, that's all." I get up from the table and hope he'll figure that's the end of the conversation.

"You'd better not be seeing him," Frankie warns. "He's not your type."

"What would *you* know about what *my* type is?"

"What's the matter with this guy, Frankie?" my father asks.

"There's *nothing* wrong with him," I say quickly, but Frankie has already started telling them that Jeremy is in tight with all the known drug dealers in the north end.

"*Drug dealers?* Oh my God!" my mother says, horrified at the thought of me having contact with the "underworld."

"It isn't true," I try to argue, as if there's any use even trying to be reasonable when they're so caught up in this big, bad gang member image that Frankie has painted.

"Well, we may not know for certain, but we can't take chances with your safety, Em," my father says in a firm voice. "Even if this Jeremy is a decent person, he is obviously a bad judge of character to be hanging around with the people that Frankie is describing. That doesn't sit well with me. I think your mother and I would prefer that you limit your association with him."

"*Limit my association?*" I ask, feeling the hair rising on the back of my neck. "What's that supposed to mean? Is that like, just see him once a week? Or just on weekends? What?"

"It means not at all," my mother says bluntly, standing next to my father so that they become a united front. "Tattoos, boys from a bad neighborhood … I don't know what's going on with you lately."

I look at my dad and he's nodding thoughtfully. This isn't the way it's supposed to be. My father is supposed to support me, argue *with* me against my mother. What's wrong with him?

"You don't even *know* him," I argue angrily. "Frankie is full of it! Why are you listening to him instead of to me? Don't you trust me?"

"Of course we trust you –" my father sighs, but I can tell by my mother's face that he isn't speaking for her.

"Then you should let me pick my own friends! He isn't even my boyfriend yet. I'm getting to know him, okay? He's just a guy, like Wyatt or Ozzie or any of Frankie's friends."

Frankie snorts and picks up his gym bag. "He's not like any of my friends. I'm a little pickier about who I spend time with."

My mother nods and waves her hand at me as if she's batting a fly away. "Emily, just move on. Find someone else to be friends with. If you've just met this boy, then it shouldn't be a big emotional thing. There are plenty of other fish in the sea –"

"*Fish in the sea?* Oh my God! That is so –" I throw my hands up in exasperation. "You're just trying to control my life. I never get to do anything I want!"

"Oh, Emily. Stop being so dramatic." My mother shakes her head and looks disappointed in me.

"Dad ...?"

He looks at me apologetically. "We have to do what's best for you. When you're a parent, you'll understand."

I choke at that and rush out of the kitchen. I run upstairs and flee down the hall, shutting myself in my bedroom. No one comes after me. I fall onto my bed, punch my pillow a few times to work out my frustration, then lie back, staring at the ceiling. Those stupid pictures of stupid models stare right back at me so I stand up on my bed and rip them all down, one after the other, flinging them onto the floor in a torn heap. When I'm finished, I fall back on my pillow and stare up at the taped corners of magazine pages still stuck to the ceiling.

There is a logical side of me that knows my parents are right when they say I barely know Jeremy, but since when does logic have anything to do with it? They're probably just jealous because they're old and dried up and can't even remember what dating is about. The fact that they are telling me that I can't see Jeremy without even bothering to get to know him is totally unfair. I expect it from my mother, but my father is usually more reasonable. I'm furious with them both, and with Frankie too.

My cell phone is lying on the bedside table. I blow my nose and pick it up to call Maddy, but then I remember that she's pissed off with me right now and that Tobi is taking her side. It would be hard to get any sympathy from them.

I call Jeremy. The phone rings a dozen times and he doesn't seem to have a message system. Irritated, I program his number into my phone, then flip it closed and put it back onto my night table. He probably isn't home yet. I'll keep trying.

I feel Grams' keys pressing through my jeans

pocket. The longer I lie there in my room, the more obvious it is to me. If my parents are going to try to stop me from seeing Jeremy, then I'll just have to meet him at Grams' place from now on. It's their own fault for not trusting me.

Leaning down, I pick up my schoolbag from the floor beside my bed. I stand up, reach into my pocket, and clutch the keys. I'll need them with me all the time now. Dropping them into my bag, I tell myself that Grams would want me to stand up for myself this way.

Chapter 6

"Your grandmother sure has a lot of stuff," Jeremy says on Monday afternoon as he walks around Grams' living room, studying the display cases.

"It just looks like a lot because it's such a small place," I tell him. There are two glass cabinets in the dining area and another in the corner of the living room, all filled with delicate china figurines, crystal, and silver. The walls are covered in paintings that Grams has collected from around the world. She never comes home from a trip abroad without something from a local artist.

"Look at this thing," he says, running a hand down the smooth surface of a Chinese vase.

"Don't touch it!" I blurt, and he is startled into drawing his hand back. "It has gold detailing on it. See? In the leaves and the petals? It's worth a fortune."

He shrugs. "I don't get it. What's the point of having all this stuff just lying around the house? Some of it is sort of … ugly." He points at a sculpture made of rock and metal.

"That's from an art show Grams took me to last year. It's a modern piece by an Inuit artist." I poke my finger into the potting soil of the philodendron in the dining room. The soil is damp, which is weird, because this is the first time I've been over.

"Looks like something even *I* could do," he comments.

I smile. "It's worth about $2,500."

"Not to me, it isn't. Just think what that kind of money could buy. Groceries, clothes, heat …"

I suddenly see Grams' cluttered home as indulgent, her collections frivolous.

"Come on. Let's watch TV," I suggest. The place is as good as ours for the next two months and I don't want to spend it thinking about my family.

Unfortunately, a picture over the television catches his attention. "Didn't you tell me that your mom and dad were split?"

I roll my eyes. "Yeah. But Grams has this idea that they'll get back together, so she's kept their picture on the wall. It drives my mom crazy when she comes over."

"They look like they're doing a commercial for those strips that make your teeth white."

"That was in their happier days."

He nods toward a picture of Frankie and me goofing around on the beach. "Hey! Is that your brother?"

"Yup, that's the Frankster."

"I know him! From baseball."

"He knows you too." I watch him pick up a carved rhinoceros. "What about your family?"

He pats the carving a few times until I reach out and take it from him, putting it back on the shelf carefully. "My dad left when I was two, so it's just my mom and me, not that she's around much." I look at him questioningly, but he doesn't go into detail. "And there's Jill."

"Who's Jill? Your sister?"

"Yeah." He hesitates. "My twin, actually. She's been living with my aunt and uncle in Albany for the last couple of years."

"Oh." It seems strange that she moved away from home when she was my age. I want to ask more about her, but I get the feeling that I shouldn't. Maybe she wasn't allowed to see the boy she liked, I think wryly. I push it out of my mind and reach up to put my arms around Jeremy's neck.

"You know what we should do after high school?" I ask. "Just bum our way around the country, staying in hostels, or sleeping on the beach. Wouldn't that be cool?"

"Yeah, but I graduate this year. By the time you're done high school, I'll be working." He kisses my neck.

"Aren't you going to college?"

He almost laughs. "Not everyone has parents who can pay for school. So, what are you going to study?"

"I don't know." I'm a little embarrassed to admit that I don't have a clue what I intend to do with my life. My parents have always said that I have to go to university, and I've never really questioned it. But that was before, when they were together, when we were the perfect family. It feels like now, those plans don't mean anything.

I pick up the remote and turn on the TV, but Jeremy takes it from me and turns it off. We settle into Grams' couch as if it's our own. I don't feel the least bit guilty about it. If anyone would understand, it's Grams. Besides, we don't actually go all the way.

At five, I tell Jeremy that I need to get home before my mother does. "Otherwise, she'll wonder what I've been up to," I say with a naughty smile. I send him out first so that it isn't obvious that we're together. I watch from the front window as he saunters up the street. He always walks slowly, with a swagger, as though he has nowhere to be.

My heart does a little flip as I think about how we have agreed to meet here again tomorrow. And the day after that …

✶✶✶

I've figured out why Grams' plants are already watered when I show up – Frankie told me that Mom has been dropping by after work sometimes to check up on the place, as though I can't be trusted to keep a few plants healthy. She's probably been going through the garbage to look for condoms and beer bottles. She'd love to catch me doing *something*, but I always make sure Jeremy and I are out of here (and any traces of us are out of here) before she's finished work.

We are lying on Grams' couch after school,

as we've so often done over the past three weeks we've been together. I am trying to ignore the fact that the Whitestrips picture of my parents has been grinning across the room at us the whole time we've been making out.

Between kisses, Jeremy asks me casually if I want to go with him to hang with the guys. This is the first time he has suggested I meet *any*one in his life, so it seems like a big deal to me. I am realizing from things he has said, or *not* said, that Jeremy may have a lot of baggage, and it has begun to worry me a little.

I know from what he's told me that the "guys" are B.B. Lawrence and his friends. I also know that hanging out with them probably means standing around on a street corner or in the parking lot of a convenience store in the north end of town. Although being invited to meet them seems like a step forward in our relationship, I can still feel myself getting nervous. I can't help thinking of what Frankie and Tobi have told me about them. Maybe I shouldn't go. My mother will be home tonight. If I want to turn him down, I can simply tell him right now that I can't get away. But I don't.

"I guess," I say, trying to keep my voice as casual as his.

"I'll meet you at the end of your street, by the bakery," he tells me. "Seven thirty. We can take a bus from the corner."

"If I'm not there, just go ahead," I say, wondering what excuse I can give my mother. She doesn't like me going out on school nights on my own. She always drives me, like I'm twelve or something.

He tousles my hair with a knowing grin on his face. "Don't worry – you'll think of something to tell your mom."

He's right. By the time I get home, I have prepared an excuse for my mother. "Lori Barrington is having a jewelry party," I tell her casually. "One of those things where they sell earrings and necklaces. I don't really want to go, but she practically begged me. She said she had to have at least ten people there to get a bonus for hosting."

"Can someone else give you a ride? I'm really tired. I was hoping to just take a bath and go to bed."

If I weren't so nervous about going, I'd be thinking about how perfect this is. "Sure. Lori's cousin said she could take us."

"Is Maddy going?" She is already heading upstairs. "We hardly ever see her anymore," she calls over her shoulder.

"I don't think so. She and Lori don't know each other all that well." I hear the water start running into the tub and a moment later, my mother comes back down the stairs and plugs in the kettle.

"Did she tell you that she and Frankie are dating?" she asks me with a smile.

"What? Maddy and Frankie are *going out*? No!" I quickly realize that my mother will wonder why news like that hasn't been shared with me. She knows as well as I do that Maddy has wanted to go out with Frankie forever. I try to bring my level of surprise down a notch. "I haven't seen her for a while."

"I hope she hasn't been sick," she says with concern. "Talk to Frankie. I think they're going to a movie tomorrow night."

I shudder. "I think it's weird. She's practically his sister."

My mother laughs and gives me a quick squeeze before making herself some tea. "Sometimes those are the best relationships. The ones where you already know someone really well."

"I guess," I say unconvincingly. I notice that the clock on the stove says it's 6:45. "I'm just going to get ready to go. I should be back by ten thirty."

"Okay. Try to be quiet coming in. I'll be in bed early."

"Sure." I head up the stairs and am passing Frankie's room when I see him sitting at his computer. I go in and he minimizes his screen so I can't see what he's doing.

"Mom just told me about you and Maddy," I tell him gloomily, dropping onto the side of his bed.

"So, what's wrong with that? She's been sending me signals for a long time. I just thought I'd check it out."

"'Check it out'? What's that supposed to mean?" I frown at him. "She isn't somebody you can just try on for size. She has feelings, you know."

He looks at me with a smirk. "Like *you* care! You're the one who stole a guy out from under her! Jeremy Mathews ..." He shakes his head as if he can't believe it.

"You don't know what you're talking about," I say, getting up from the bed to leave.

"Oh, I don't? Like I don't know that you've been seeing him? Or that you've been lying to Mom and Dad about it?"

"Screw you," I tell him, at a loss to come up

with anything more suitable.

"Good one," he answers sarcastically. "The point is, you're a lousy friend. You don't give a shit about Maddy or what she feels. She's been really hurt because you would rather see Jeremy than be her friend." I must look stunned because he adds, "She needs *some*one to talk to on the way home." I realize that she and Frankie must have been walking home together while I was meeting Jeremy after school.

"She's still my best friend," I insist. "And she's had a crush on you since she was twelve. If you hurt her –" It hits me how much I miss her.

"I'm just taking her to a movie!" he says with frustration. "What's your problem? I think she's cute, okay?"

"You knew her when she had braces on her teeth. And she knew you when you were a walking ad for zit cream. She's even seen you in the morning when your hair is sticking out sideways and your breath is bad. The whole idea of you guys together is just gross."

"Like we care what you think," he says, turning away from me and tapping the computer keys restlessly. "Close my door on your way out."

"It's like *incest*," I hiss and slam his door behind me.

I know them both too well to think that this can ever work. Maddy will be sensitive and vulnerable when it comes to Frankie. I think about how upset she was when Jon Willson broke up with her. That would be nothing compared to this.

Frankie is probably just amusing himself, going out with Maddy because he's flattered by her crush on him. He is way more experienced than she is, and I hate to think that his idea of "trying it out" has anything to do with getting Maddy into bed. For her own good, I have to keep them from getting together in the first place. I just need to come up with a way to keep them apart.

While changing my jeans and pulling on a skinny ribbed sweater, I toy with ideas. I could leave some of the worst pictures I have of Maddy lying around for him to see. There's the one of her wearing her brother's hockey sweater on seventh-grade picture day. And the one when she'd had her hair cut really short and her ears looked huge. Trouble is, Frankie knew her through those phases and it doesn't seem to have bothered him.

After saying goodbye to my mother through the bathroom door, I hurry down the stairs. As I pass by the hall table, I see Frankie's cell phone next to the vase of dried flowers. It suddenly dawns on me how I can keep Maddy from her date with my brother.

I pick up the phone and start punching the keys. "Made other plans 4 fri – maybe sum other time. F."

Maddy will be furious and will never want to see him again. Better mad than hurt, I figure.

I toss the phone back onto the table and glance at myself in the hall mirror. Brushing my hair back with my fingers, I squint at myself. I pull the lip gloss from my pocket and touch up my lips nervously. *You're going to a street corner to hang out with a bunch of guys that everyone says are thugs. Do you really think that lip gloss matters?*

Chapter 7

"Here she is. This is Emily." I can tell from the way Jeremy says it that he has told them about me before. I say hello and Jeremy introduces them one at a time. Owen. Bing. Wes and Dion. A couple more names that I don't catch right away.

"And this big guy is B.B.," Jeremy tells me, pointing toward the guy leaning against the wall of the convenience store. He is the size of a football player and heavy, but he has movements that are smooth and easy. He's wearing a leather jacket with a scorpion on the chest. He's got a chain around his neck that is so thick, it can't possibly be real gold.

"So you're that girl that J was tellin' us about." He looks me over critically. "How old are you?"

"Fifteen."

"Man, you are robbing the cradle!" he says to Jeremy, and the other guys laugh. "That's jail bait!"

"I'm not that much younger than him," I say boldly, daring anyone to argue.

"Yeah. But J's the baby of this group, aren't you? Just got out of diapers last year."

"That's funny, man. Diapers," Jeremy quips. "But that's why you keep me around, 'cause you guys are getting so old and tired that the girls don't give you the time of day anymore. You need me here to get their attention." I like the way he isn't letting B.B. get to him. He seems comfortable and relaxed in his friends' company.

"You can do better than to hang with this punk," B.B. says, eyeing me with appreciation. "I'd have guessed you were older. If you were, I'd give J the signal to get lost, you know what I mean?"

They all snicker again, but I don't think it's funny. "You really think I'd be interested?" I ask him sarcastically, and everyone but B.B. practically falls to the ground laughing.

Jeremy must think this is a good time to impress everyone, so he tells them all how I'm going to be a "big-time doctor or lawyer one day," though I've never said any such thing to him, ever.

"You want to be my lawyer?" Owen asks in a cocky tone. The others start joking about how he *always* needs a lawyer and how he'd *better* get a good one or he'll end up doing time one of these days. I feel really uncomfortable, but Jeremy is still smiling and joking with them. I guess they're just kidding around about Owen being in trouble.

We stay there for about an hour, while I try to act as though I am not feeling *totally* out of place. I'm talking to Owen when he suddenly stiffens and looks past me down the street. I turn to follow his eyes and see that a police car is approaching from down the block. Owen tosses his cigarette to the ground and goes into the convenience store. The rest of them just watch the car as it slows and passes us at half speed. The two officers in the cruiser both look over and scan our faces, pausing on mine for a moment too long. I look away. They speed up slightly after passing us and continue down the street.

Everyone laughs and starts joking around, and Owen comes back out. No one seems to care that they've just been checked out as if they're criminals or something. But *I* care. I feel guilty, even though I've done nothing but stand in a public place. I want to go home. Now.

Jeremy must notice my discomfort. "Do you want to go?" he asks me, and I nod and say we should think about leaving soon. I still have lots of time, but I just want to get away from here. People going in and out of the store look at us sideways or start to walk faster, and I'm embarrassed to be seen as part of the group. Although my parents' friends aren't likely to come to this neighborhood, I'm still worried that someone I know might see me.

"Just gimme a minute," Jeremy tells me. He and B.B. move away from the group, talking quietly at the side of the building. I'm sure that I see B.B. give a stack of money to Jeremy. He takes it and puts it into his pocket. He walks back over to me without a word. I can feel the hair rising on my arms. I swallow nervously, wondering what the money is for and why they had to exchange it in private. I immediately decide I don't want to know anything about it. "Nice meeting you guys," I say, as Jeremy and I turn to walk slowly away.

"Hey! Our pleasure!" B.B. calls after me, and then one of them says "My, my!" They all laugh, and I wonder if they are watching me as I'm walking. Jeremy turns and gives them the finger and they all laugh some more.

"They're all pigs," Jeremy tells me, putting his arm around me so his hand rests on my hip, as it always does when we walk together.

"But you like them," I note.

"Yeah. They're family," he says. I'm glad they aren't *my* family.

I am grateful to be moving again; the temperature has dropped considerably and my feet had gotten cold just standing outside the store in my sandals. Jeremy takes my hand and we walk together quietly under the streetlights. I'm glad he's with me or I'd be uncomfortable in this neighborhood.

As we head along unfamiliar streets, I can't help but wonder why Jeremy would want to hang out with a group of older guys who seem to do nothing but stand around and intimidate people passing by. Sometimes I think that I don't know anything at all about Jeremy or about his life.

"Do you want to go to my place?" he asks me unexpectedly. "It isn't late."

I look at him with surprise. He has never taken me to his house or introduced me to his mother. This is the perfect opportunity to get to know her. "Sure. I'd like that."

We walk several more minutes, then head onto a street of older homes and unkempt apartment buildings. Eventually, we turn into an empty driveway. The house is small with a concrete front stoop and green shutters that even in this light are in obvious need of painting.

The front door is not locked. As we step into the small front hallway, I'm disappointed to realize that there's no one home. The front room is cold for late May. The house is furnished sparsely. There is a stack of unopened mail on the floor beside the front door. I step into the living room and can see the empty kitchen, dirty plates in the sink. "Where's your mom?" I ask.

"I don't know. Probably at her boyfriend's. She spends a lot of time there." We go into the kitchen and he grabs us each a Coke from an almost-empty fridge. I take the can from him and wander a few steps over to the bookcases that line one wall of the living room. There are pictures on the shelves, mostly school photos, covered in dust.

"Who's this?" I ask. A girl about thirteen or fourteen is smiling at the camera. He comes to stand beside me. "That's Jill. Seven minutes older than me. She's pretty, huh?"

Although she has Jeremy's slight build, it's hard to believe they are twins. Her hair is much thicker, wilder, and her eyes are more gray than blue.

"Yeah. She looks as if she's really nice too." I put the picture back and peer at what I assume is a wedding picture of his parents. They both look stiff in their formal wedding attire. Neither of them are smiling. I can see that Jeremy looks most like his mother, while Jill looks more like her father. "When did you say Jill moved?"

"A couple of years ago." His face twitches uncomfortably. "She'd had enough of this town."

"Yeah, I can relate to that," I say, rolling my eyes. "There are plenty of times when I'd like to run off too."

"She likes it in Albany," he continues, smiling a little as he thinks of his sister. "And she's doing real good at school. She's going to go to college next year to become a dental hygienist." He shakes his head in wonder.

I look around and try to imagine his life in this house. The living room is depressingly run-down, the carpet worn, the windows bare. "Did you ever think of moving there with her?"

"Yeah, I have. It's gotta be better there."

It would have to be. At least they would have heat. He sees me shiver. "Sorry. It's kind of cold in here." He gets up and goes to the front closet, returning with a scarf that he wraps around my shoulders. I thank him, as I roll my hands into the ends. He has left the closet door open and I catch sight of a guitar standing against the wall inside.

"Is that yours?"

He looks over to see what I am talking about and then turns back sheepishly. "Yeah, my uncle gave it to me last year. I'm not that good. I never took lessons or anything." He goes over to the closet and pulls out the old guitar. He holds it out to me as he heads back to the couch.

"I can't believe you never told me that you play the guitar," I say incredulously, turning it over in my hands and toying with the strings tunelessly.

"I didn't say I could play it well."

"Play something for me. And sing."

"I'm not much of a singer."

He takes the guitar from me, strums a bit as though he needs to get a feel for it, then starts into a song that I don't recognize. His voice is soft. He's better than he lets on.

"You know who you sound like? John Mayer!"

"I doubt it, but thanks." He leans over and kisses me. "I'd write you a song – if I was good enough."

Just saying he'd like to is enough. If I block out everything else – the warnings from my family, his questionable friends, the cold empty house, the rift between me and Maddy – then I can almost believe that Jeremy is the right person for me. But even as he is sitting next to me, playing his guitar and looking so sweet and so untroubled, I know that all those other things still matter to me.

When it's time to head home, Jeremy walks me to the bus terminal. We stand on the platform and kiss until the #17 bus arrives. "I wish you didn't have to go home," he says.

"I could wait for the next bus," I suggest, but I have hesitated and he knows it.

"No, that's okay. It's just –" his mouth twists in an embarrassed smile. "I liked having you at the house. It gets kind of lonely when my mom is away."

"Away? You mean her boyfriend's place is out of town?"

He nods. "She hasn't been home since Sunday."

"That's four days ago!"

"It's no big deal. Sometimes she's gone for weeks."

"Jesus, Jeremy. That's a long time to be alone."

He looks at me as if I'm naïve. "I'm seventeen. I don't need her to take care of me. *I've* always taken care of *her*."

"But she isn't even home," I point out. I think about the empty shelves of the old refrigerator. "You can't live like that. It isn't fair." I hug him tightly.

The bus is ready to leave so I reluctantly board, turning to wave from the steps as the doors close. Sliding into a seat by the window, I watch as he waits on the platform. The bus pulls away, and I see him walk back down the street, his shoulders slumped and his steps heavy, with no trace of his trademark swagger.

Chapter 8

On the way home, the stench of diesel fuel and the sway of the half-empty bus makes me slightly nauseated. I close my eyes and think of Jeremy's bleak house and his absent mother. I realize how much I care about him and want to help him.

The bus drops me off and I walk through my neighborhood and up the path to my back door, actually feeling grateful to be home.

When I get upstairs, I see a light beneath my mother's bedroom door. As I pass, I hear quiet sobs. "Mom?" I ask, tapping lightly. "Are you okay?"

"Come in," she sniffs. She's in the middle of the bed, wiping at her eyes with her fingers, a pile of old greeting cards and letters spread across the comforter. She looks as though she's in mourning. "I'm trying to figure out why I bother to keep all these," she says, gesturing at the mess in front of her. I pick up a card and glance inside. It's an old birthday card from my dad to her, telling her how much he loves her. It makes me feel a little guilty for what I've been doing to her lately.

"I've kept them all," she admits. "But there just doesn't seem to be much of a point now, does there?" She picks up a sheet of paper and reads it to herself, her lips quivering. "Poetry," she says. "He loved to write me poetry."

"Why are you doing this to yourself?" I ask gently, brushing the cards and letters together into a pile. I sit on the bed beside her. "Put them away. Or burn them. Don't sit and wallow in them."

"He's going to start dating," she tells me. "He called me today to let me know. He didn't want me to hear about it from someone else."

"Well, that's good, right?" I suggest, feeling that it is anything but good. "I mean, he's moving on. That's what you both need to do."

"I know. *I know.* But that doesn't mean that it's easy. I had no way of knowing that it would hit me so hard. I feel like he's leaving me."

"Mom, you kicked him out. You wanted to be on your own."

She shakes her head. "I still feel like he's supposed to be there for me." She takes a slow deep breath. "What an idiot I am."

"You're not an idiot, Mom."

"Your Grams thinks I made a mistake, asking him to leave. She thinks we should have tried harder to work things out. Maybe she was right."

"And maybe not. You and Dad are like polar opposites, remember?"

She looks down for a moment. "So, where have you been? Tobi dropped by about an hour ago looking for you, and she didn't know anything about Lori's jewelry party."

I can't believe that Tobi would come over now, of all times. She hasn't been over for weeks. Even though we've been speaking to each other at school, whenever I mention Jeremy, she still gets a pinched look on her face.

"So where were you?"

I push a few of the letters back into a stack and pull my feet up on the bed, tucking them under me. I could lie again, but I am actually grateful for the chance to talk. "I was at Jeremy's."

"Jeremy? That boy we told you not to see?" I expect her to be furious, but her face is more disappointed than angry. She's on an emotional low and anger would take too much energy right now.

I nod. "I like him. He's really nice, and I don't think anybody gave him a chance ..."

"And you've been seeing him behind my back," she says.

I try to keep my voice level. I don't want to argue with her. Not now. "I didn't want to go behind your back. It's just that we didn't have much choice."

"Of course you had a choice. The choice was either to continue seeing him after being told not to, or to listen to us and find someone more suitable." She's gaining momentum. I've given her something to think about other than Dad dating.

"He's not a horrible person, Mom." I search for things to say to make her understand. "He opens doors for me. He respects me. He has a good sense of humor. He's honest."

"Has he been honest about what he's doing with those boys he hangs around with?" She leans forward with her arms folded. "Has he told you whether they're involved with drugs?"

I think again about the exchange of money that I had witnessed earlier. It has been bothering me, but I won't let myself believe that Jeremy is involved with anything illegal. "I never asked. And besides, whatever it is they might do, he isn't like them."

"Then why does he hang out with them?" she asks.

I feel a fleeting doubt. "I don't know. They grew up in the same neighborhood. It's like they're connected."

"They aren't in a gang, are they?" She's talking as if she knows everything.

"You watch too much TV," I suggest, and she huffs. I take a deep breath. I had started talking to her for a reason and I may as well keep going. "He's just, I don't know, it seems like he's kind of in trouble. His house is cold. And there was hardly anything in the fridge – just some Cokes and pizza. I'm worried about him."

"I knew he wasn't someone you should be involved with –"

"Mom! That's horrible! His home life isn't *his* fault!" My eyes are burning and I can feel my cheeks flush.

She is silent for a moment. "What about his family?"

"It's just him and his mother, and she's away a lot. Sometimes for days."

"Days?" I can see her concern growing.

"He has a twin sister, but she lives in Albany with an aunt and uncle."

"Why doesn't he live there too?"

It feels like a criticism. "Jeremy stayed home to be with his mother."

"Who is never home. And she must not have a job or she wouldn't disappear like that." My mother thinks that people can be lumped into three categories: working, retired, or milking the system. I can tell by her tone that my mother has already placed her in the last group.

"I don't know. Jeremy doesn't talk about her much." I picture him walking away from the bus terminal. "He just seems so sad."

"You're not just seeing him because you feel sorry for him, are you?" she asks, studying my face.

"No! Of course not."

She sighs. "Tell you what," she says, rubbing my knee. "Let's have him over for supper on Friday night. I'll try to get to know him better. Maybe I didn't give him enough of a chance."

She actually sounds reasonable, and I'm so relieved to have finished arguing that I agree without thinking about the implications. "Thanks, Mom." I stand and look at the mess of papers on her bed. "Are you going to be okay?"

"I'm fine." She scoops everything into a big pile and picks up a bag from the floor. "Knowing that you've been seeing that boy has managed to distract me."

"Jeremy. His name is Jeremy."

"Yes. Jeremy." She shoves her cards and letters into the bag, looking exhausted.

I leave and head for my room. Frankie calls out to me and I poke my head into his bedroom. He has a picture of Maddy taped to his computer screen. It's her class picture from last year, the one that used to be stuck on my bedroom mirror.

"Tobi was here," he tells me, turning away from the computer.

"I know. Mom told me."

"I guess she and Maddy have decided to forgive you for being a jerk. Even after that text message. What a dumb-ass move! We had a good laugh over it though."

"I'm glad you all think I'm so funny."

I make a haughty exit and go to my room to call Jeremy. I invite him for dinner and he agrees to come. I'm still feeling good about it when my phone rings. Tobi's number is on the call display.

"Hi, Tobi."

"Hi! Did your mom tell you I was there?

"Yeah. Sorry I missed you."

"Did Lori have a jewelry party and not invite me?"

"No. I just told my mom that story so I could get out of the house for a little while."

"Oh, well, I need to talk to you about Maddy's birthday. It's only a couple of weeks away and we need to start planning that surprise party for her."

I don't admit it, but with everything that's been going on I had completely forgotten that Tobi and I had talked about having a party for Maddy. I feel a little guilty for not having thought of it since our falling out.

"Are you sure she'd even want me there?" I ask doubtfully.

She sighs. "You guys have been friends forever and it's stupid to let Jeremy come between you. Or us. Besides, she's pretty much over it now, especially since she started going out with Frankie – "

"Yeah. What's with that?" I ask, sitting on the edge of my bed, relieved to be talking normally to Tobi again. "You know what he's like. He's a player – he'll never get serious about her."

"I don't know. I think he's changed. He actually left a rose taped to the front of her locker yesterday."

"A rose? Are you kidding me? Are you talking about *my* brother Frankie, the one whose idea of a date is to split the cost of a pizza and then try to get the girl into bed?"

She laughs. "I think he really likes her. He's already asked me what to buy her for her birthday."

"All he gave me for my birthday were some free discount coupons that he picked up at the bowling alley," I remind her.

"You're his sister. He doesn't need to impress you."

"I wish he'd try." I think about Maddy's birthday and how I can help with the party. Suddenly, I get a brilliant idea. "You know what? We could have the party at my Grams' place." I guess it's my way of apologizing to Tobi and Maddy for the past few weeks.

"I don't know," she answers doubtfully. "Is it big enough? I don't know if everyone will fit."

"It'll be fine! Maddy will be totally surprised because she'd never expect it to be there. Besides, if we had it at your house, we'd have your little brothers running around, and at my house we'd have my mother doing a liquor check every five minutes."

"That's true."

"Come on! Let me do this for Maddy."

She finally gives in. "Okay. Your Grams'

place it is."

"I'd better try calling Maddy, you know, to sort of make up."

"You probably should. After all, she'll be at your place Friday night for supper, right? Your mom invited her over."

My stomach tightens. That's the same night that Jeremy's coming.

I hang up and wonder if a peaceful meal is even possible for Friday. I decide to suck it up and just call her.

Maddy answers, even though she has call display and knows it's me. That's a good start. I tell her that I feel like shit about everything that has happened and that I really want for us to be friends again. As she tells me how much she has missed me too, I realize that Tobi is right – having Frankie finally ask her out seems to have changed everything.

When I explain that my mother has invited her and Jeremy for the same evening, Maddy barely gives it a second thought. I can only hope that she is being honest when she says that she is ready to face Jeremy again.

Chapter 9

When the doorbell rings on Friday night, I stop setting the table and go to answer it. I see Maddy through the narrow glass pane in the door and I smile at her.

"Hi," I say, standing back so she can come in. "You didn't have to ring the bell."

"I didn't know if I was still allowed to just walk in," she answers sheepishly. "I'm sort of here as Frankie's girlfriend now and, you know, it's different." I can see that she feels as unsure about herself as I feel about myself. *Some*one has to make the first move.

"But you're still *my* friend too, and I've missed you so much!" I say, throwing my arms around her, practically knocking her over. After we hug, she steps back and stands awkwardly. "Look, Maddy. I really meant it when I told you I was sorry about Jeremy. He and I just clicked and –"

She waves off my apology. "It's okay. Really. I knew that he wasn't going to be right for me. Frankie is the only guy I've ever really been crazy about. You know that."

"Yeah, that's why I took Jeremy out of play. I was *trying* to pave the way for Frankie to ask you out," I giggle.

"Oh, you're too good!" She kicks off her shoes and glances into the living room for him.

"Frankie's just shaving. He'll be down in a minute." I've no sooner said it than he comes down the stairs. There's a small piece of Kleenex stuck to his face where he has cut himself with his razor.

"Nice touch," I say, peeling it off and handing it to him. Maddy and I both crack up as Frankie wipes at the cut in embarrassment.

Jeremy shows up a few minutes later and sits with Maddy and Frankie in the living room, while I help my mother with dinner. There are long silences and I think everyone is relieved when I finally call them to the table.

Even though Maddy told me she wouldn't

mind sitting through dinner with Jeremy, it's obvious that she's ignoring him. When he asks her a question, she answers with a yes or no, then turns to Frankie and changes the subject. My mother is trying desperately to make up for it by inanely chatting about anything and everything. Frankie keeps smirking at me from across the table and every now and again, he taps or scratches his head in an obvious reference to Jeremy's hair, which is longer than ever.

"It's been ages since you were here, Maddy," my mother chirps as she passes the roast potatoes. "I was starting to worry that you and Emily had had a falling out." I blush and lean over my plate so that no one will notice.

"I've just been busy," Maddy says graciously.

"You'll be seeing more of her from now on," Frankie promises, giving Maddy's shoulders an affectionate squeeze. She reacts by smiling at him adoringly. I smile too, but my expression is more pained. The two of them are giving me gas.

"What movie are you going to see tonight?" Jeremy asks, looking at the embroidered linen napkin before wiping his mouth on it.

"Whatever Maddy chooses," Frankie answers. My mouth practically falls open. Frankie *always* chooses the movie. His girlfriends have always complained that he only wants to see action or horror films.

"Who *are* you?" I hope that Maddy picks the sappiest chick flick in the theater.

"He has to let me choose," Maddy laughs, and she finally sounds more like the Maddy that I've always known. "I'm paying." That explains it. She gives me a look that says *I know – I'm a sucker.*

Jeremy takes a second helping of chicken before starting to talk to Frankie about football – which players are overpaid and which team will win the Super Bowl next year. But then Frankie looks at Jeremy kind of slyly. "So, what made you quit baseball?"

"Broken ankle," Jeremy explains. "It never healed properly. Still hurts sometimes."

"Oh, yeah? I thought maybe you couldn't make the team."

"Frankie!" my mother gasps.

Jeremy smiles slowly and then pulls down his sock right there at the dinner table and shows us where the pins have been placed on both sides of his ankle. He had never shown me that before. No one says a word as he pulls his sock back up and settles back into his chair.

"So, Jer, I understand you're a friend of

Owen Mitchell's?" Frankie is looking across the table with feigned innocence.

My blood goes cold. Jeremy raises his eyebrows. "Sure I know him. Why?"

"I heard he got picked up last night. Assault charges." Frankie is serving himself more vegetables and acting as if this is a totally casual conversation. But everyone can see that he knows exactly what he's doing.

"Assault charges?" my mother says, looking up from her plate. I could kill Frankie.

"Where did you hear that?" Jeremy asks, putting his fork down.

"From some guys I know."

"So you know guys who hang with Owen?" Jeremy asks pointedly.

Frankie looks at him with surprise, recognizes the implication, and then smiles slowly. "I guess I do."

"Small world," Jeremy says as he picks up his fork. Point made. My mother is looking back and forth between the two boys uncomfortably.

"How's your sister?" Frankie goes on. "She moved away, right?"

"Yeah. A couple of years ago."

"Huh." With that one sound, Frankie manages to say a mouthful. I wish he'd choke on his food.

"We should be going soon," Maddy suggests in an obvious effort to end the exchange. "Can I help clear some of these dishes, Mrs. Talifer?" She is already on her feet, picking up her plate.

My mother waves a hand at her. "No, no. Just leave them there, Maddy. Em and I will get them after you go."

"I'll help," Jeremy says, standing and taking my plate and his own.

"Do you need tips or something?" Frankie sneers.

"Frankie! That's enough!"

"Just kidding, Mom. I was only going to say that I'm not much of a tipper."

"No surprise there," I say. "Don't forget you still owe me twenty bucks from last week."

"What for?" my mother asks.

"I needed a haircut. You can relate to that, right Jer?" Frankie is straight across the table from me, so I kick his shin. He doesn't even flinch.

Jeremy doesn't miss a beat. "I'm letting this grow until I can tie it back. Not that the whole shaved-head look that you've got going on doesn't suit you. It's just not for me."

"We have hair clippers upstairs if you want to take a crack at it," Frankie offers.

"I think short hair is nice," Maddy adds, running a hand quickly over Frankie's bare head.

"See why I like her?" Frankie grins. I wait until he has risen from the table, then turn to Jeremy and make a gagging gesture.

When they have left for the movies, Jeremy helps my mother and me clean up the dishes.

"So, are you ready for your exams, Jeremy?" my mother asks. They don't start until the week of Maddy's party, but she's been at me about it already. I guess she figures someone needs to bother him about it too.

"Not yet. There's lots of time."

"It's never too soon to study," she reproaches. Then she tries to draw him into a conversation about his home. The more questions she asks, the more withdrawn he becomes. When she finds out that his mother doesn't work, my mother asks point blank if she's interested in working. "I know of a position coming available in our packing department. I could try to help her get a foot in the door."

"That's nice of you, but I'd really rather not talk about my mother," he says, turning and tossing a dishcloth into the sink.

"Oh. All right." My mother gives the countertop a quick wipe with the tea towel. "Well,

I should get some work done." She goes into her office just down the hall.

"I guess I should be leaving," Jeremy says to me, turning and starting down the hall before I can object. He walks past Mom's office to the front door and slips his shoes on. "This was a good idea, my getting to know your family. It sort of put things into perspective for me."

"Frankie was awful. He was jabbing at you the entire time."

"It's okay. He's just trying to watch out for you. That's what brothers do." He smiles a bit, then looks down at his shoes uncomfortably. "You know, Em, I've been thinking –"

"Oh, no! Not thinking!" I joke, but I really don't like the way he said it.

He doesn't laugh. His voice drops. "I really like you, but we're different. Frankie just laid it on the line for me. He's a rich kid on the baseball team and I'm some slob from the north end who can't afford a hair cut. He doesn't think I'm good enough for you, and maybe I'm not. Your mother was making it pretty clear too, asking all those questions …"

"Who cares what they think?" I put my arms around his neck and hug him.

"But we *are* different. I'm living on whatever

my mother can dig up at the end of the month. You live in this big house – "

"It's not that big," I interrupt as I look around at the entranceway and into our living room. It's as though I'm seeing it for the first time. It's freaking huge.

"You've got all the advantages, and you'll go to university and be a lawyer or something –"

My voice bristles. "Where did you get that from?"

"I just know. You're that kind of person. You're smart and you care about people, and your parents expect it of you."

"I don't have to do what my parents want," I tell him defiantly. "I've got my own mind, you know. If I'd listened to them, I would never have gone out with you in the first place."

He colors a bit. "Yeah."

I realize how that sounded and hug him tightly, hoping he'll stop thinking about it. He eventually hugs me back and strokes my hair. "Are you okay?" I ask.

"Sure. Yeah." We kiss and then he turns away and heads for the open doorway of Mom's office. "Thanks for dinner, Mrs. Talifer," he says to my mother, who sits keying frantically at her computer as if to prove that she hasn't been listening to everything we've said.

"I hope you'll come again," my mother offers. She looks at him with what appears to be sympathy.

I kiss Jeremy goodbye, right there in front of her, and then he leaves.

"Do you want to talk?" my mother calls to me. I just turn and run upstairs to my room. I should never have let him come to the house for dinner. I should have known that Mom and Frankie would ruin everything. I don't know what I was thinking.

Chapter 10

Even though Jeremy said he was fine, things have changed. He has been hard to reach for the past two weeks, he's come up with weak excuses for not seeing me, and he's only come to meet me at Grams' place once. He said he would try to make it to Maddy's birthday party, but it started almost an hour ago and he hasn't shown yet.

More and more people are coming through the door. There must be about thirty people here already. I try to convince myself that I don't care – that everything will be fine.

"I thought Jeremy would be here by now," Tobi says loudly over the noise.

"He said he might come later." I catch myself watching the entrance, hoping to see him walk in.

A loud crash in the kitchen distracts me and I dart off, leaving Tobi to answer the door.

"It's just a vase," my friend Lucas shrugs, pointing to the mess on the kitchen floor. "Sorry! These ceramic floors really make stuff shatter, don't they?" I groan and hand him a broom and dustpan.

I go into the living room in time to see that someone has knocked over a beer. Donnie is trying to wipe it off the carpet with one of Grams' antique lace doilies. Rick has his feet up on the walnut coffee table. Grams' things are being moved around the room haphazardly to make space for everyone. Ozzie nearly fell against the china cabinet because the room is getting so packed with people. I've lost track of all the things that are going wrong. If we can survive this without a major disaster, I'll be surprised. I decide I'll just try to keep it from getting *too* out of hand, and if I have to spend the next week cleaning up, then that's what I'll do.

"Maddy's here!" someone calls from near the front window. "They're parking the car right now." There is a lot of giggling and scrambling for positions.

I soon hear Frankie's voice in the hallway outside, then Maddy's, and I wonder how it is possible that they can't hear Jessica telling her boyfriend to stop tickling her or Ozzie complaining that he wants to put the music back on. A cell phone rings in someone's pocket and a collective groan of disgust fills the room, followed by laughter. It is impossible to remain quiet.

A key turns in the lock and Frankie opens the door. "What's going on?" Maddy asks, stepping into the room.

"Surprise!" most of us yell in unison, watching her face in anticipation.

"Oh, my God!" she says, putting her hands up to her face. It's an act. I can tell that she already knew about the party because she is wearing brand new jeans, a new fitted T-shirt, and the leather jacket that she told me she had been planning to buy.

There's a lot of talking going on all at once, and plenty of reassurances from Maddy that she had no idea that everyone would be here. Eventually Ozzie turns the music back up and we go back to partying. I tell myself to lighten up as I try to ignore the drinking and the smoking. I'll just have to find some major air freshener.

The party is in full swing an hour later when I make my way across the living room to talk to Maddy. "Where's Frankie?" I ask over the music.

"He just went to get my present," Maddy answers excitedly. She's talking about what Frankie may have bought her when we hear a startled cry and a heavy thud on the stairwell to the condo, followed by a string of swearwords.

We rush out to see Frankie cursing with pain. "Oh my God! Frankie!" Maddy races frantically down the stairs to his side, and we all pour after her to help. Frankie holds up his hand to keep everyone away.

"Some idiot spilled something on the stairs. I think I broke my friggin' arm," he says through gritted teeth, sitting up and gently cradling his right arm as he winces. A gift bag is lying on its side next to him.

"It's too bad you weren't drinking, man. You might've bounced," Ozzie laughs. Neither Frankie nor Ozzie are drinking. Their baseball coach has threatened to kick anyone off the team if they so much as touch a beer bottle during the season.

"I'll call an ambulance," I say worriedly, but Frankie shakes his head.

"Ozzie's sober – he can drive us to the hospital," he says. "It's not like I need a stretcher. I'm okay except for the arm."

"Want me to call Mom?" I ask.

"I guess so," he says reluctantly. "She's going to make a big deal out of this, isn't she?"

"Of course she is. It's what she does. She'll be complaining about the lineup at emergency, and she'll demand to see whoever is in charge, and she'll cry and tell everyone there that you're such a good boy, and so brave –"

"Oh God. Maybe you should call Dad instead."

"I'll call them both," I say. He looks unsure. "If I don't, they'll think I'm playing favorites. But I'm not going to tell them where we are. They think we're having a nice supervised party at Tobi's house. I'll tell them to meet us at the hospital."

Chapter 11

We flow into the emergency reception area like an entourage accompanying a rock star: Frankie is in front, holding his arm immobile against his chest, and Maddy is walking by his side with her hand on his lower back, as though she's ushering him forward. I'm on his other side, shielding him from people and swinging doors, and Ozzie, who had been our chauffeur, is trailing behind.

Mom and Dad are both there already. When Mom sees us, she leaps to her feet and takes over, ensuring that a nurse knows "the" patient has arrived. Frankie is taken into an examining room, with my mother by his side. Ozzie hangs around with us in the waiting room for a few minutes, but eventually he excuses himself to go back to the party. I walk with him to the door, grabbing his arm anxiously. "Make sure that things are under control when you get back there," I hiss.

"What am I, a bouncer?" Ozzie scoffs. "It'll be fine. Don't worry so much."

"Easy for you to say," I mumble. I pull out my phone and dial Tobi.

"What's happening over there?" I ask her, turning away so that my father won't hear.

"*Em*, it's getting way out of control," Tobi answers in a shrill voice. "There are too many people, and there's all this booze – " I hear something break in the background.

"Shit! What was that?"

"Another glass. What am I supposed to do?"

"Kick everyone out!"

"Are you kidding me?" She sounds desperate.

"I'll be back as soon as I can." I hang up, take a deep breath, and go over to join my father in the waiting area.

"Maddy went in to see Frankie," my father says. "She's really worried about him, isn't she?"

"Yeah. She really cares about him." I'm just ever-so-slightly jealous of their happiness. And of the fact that my dad is so obviously happy for them.

My mom comes out and sits down beside my

dad, updating him on Frankie's condition. His arm is broken in two places, she tells us. Her eyes fill with tears and my father puts his arm around her. He lets her lean into him.

Even though it's terrible and I feel sort of guilty for thinking it, I'm almost glad that Frankie broke his arm. If only for the moment, my parents are getting along again. We sit there together, all of us lost in our own thoughts. Unfortunately, mine are mainly about that friggin' party. I wonder if my parents can see that I'm sweating.

After what seems like forever, Maddy and Frankie finally come walking out with a doctor. My parents stand and listen to the instructions for the pain medication he'll need to take, then turn to Frankie and ask if he's all set to go home.

"I don't know. The party should still be on –"

"It's *my* party, and I'm here, so it's as good as over," Maddy chides. "Go home and get some rest." We can all see that he is looking pale and worn out. I guess pain does that to a person.

"I'm sorry I screwed up your birthday," Frankie says to her, and it seems as if he really means it. The guy has gone all genuine and sensitive on us. "We'll do something else for your birthday later. Maybe go to a nice restaurant or something," he promises her.

"That'll cost you," I tell Maddy and she laughs with me. Frankie can only muster a couple of weak *ha ha*'s. If he doesn't have the strength to call me on one of my bad jokes, I know he's finished for the night.

We say goodbye to my dad, and he heads out to the parking lot.

"Let's go home too, shall we?" my mother suggests. "Maddy, we can drop you on the way." All I want is to get back to that party and break it up before anything else can happen. We are outside the hospital when Mom turns to Frankie. "What should we do about your car? I don't want to leave it on Tobi's street all night. It might get towed."

Frankie sees my panicked expression and knows we'll have a lot of explaining to do if she decides to look for his car at Tobi's house. "I already gave the keys to Ozzie. He'll drive it home for me," he lies easily.

"Oh, good," my mother says, patting his shoulder.

I look at him gratefully. Then I grab Maddy's arm and pull her back, so we're well behind Mom and Frankie. "I need to go back to the party right away," I whisper. "I called Tobi. She says it's totally out of hand."

"Oh no! But how are you going to get there? You can't get your mother to drop you off at your Grams'! People started going out front and smoking butts when we left ..."

"Okay, I've got it. Ask me to stay overnight at your place in front of my mom. She'll drop us off and I'll just run over to the condo from there.

"You? Run?" She agrees. We hustle to catch up and we all climb into Mom's car. My nerves are shot. It's all I can do not to barf as we pull out of the lot. I turn and flash Maddy a pleading look. She's sitting in the back seat with Frankie.

"Mrs. Talifer, can Em stay over at my place tonight?" Maddy asks. "We both want to help clean up over at Tobi's place in the morning."

"I guess so," my mother answers. She would never say no to Maddy.

The drive seems endless. When we finally arrive at Maddy's, the two of us hop out of the car. "See you guys," I say quickly. "I hope your arm doesn't hurt too much, Frankie."

"Thanks," he answers, knowing full well that I am heading back to the party.

"Go straight to bed," my mother says, as though I am twelve.

"Uh huh." I close the car door and she pulls away. They are barely around the corner when

Maddy says, "I'll come with you. And here – Frankie slipped me his car keys." She hands them to me.

"Good." I take them from her and slide them in my pocket. "Let's go." We both take off running toward the condo.

Ten minutes later, my breath catches as I see Donnie and Mick standing outside my grandmother's building having a cigarette. The living room window is directly above them, a light shining through the sheer draperies, people moving about behind it. The music is pumping out into the street.

"Go home," I shout at Donnie and Mick, not stopping to hear their reaction. I open the outer door and scurry up the stairs with Maddy right behind me.

"Get out. NOW!" I tell them all as I shut off the music.

"But we're just getting started," someone complains. "It's, like, only twelve thirty."

"Get out or I'll call the police!" I shout in desperation. Everyone starts gathering their things, muttering, laughing, complaining. Maddy yells at everyone about designated drivers and calling for cabs. Ozzie comes over and asks about Frankie. He tells me he tried to get people to leave earlier, but I can tell he's lying. I hand him Frankie's keys and practically demand that he drive the car to our house. At least I can count on him being sober. Ozzie realizes that now is not the time to argue with me. He arranges to have Lily, who doesn't drink, follow him in his car so that he can get home afterward.

"Ozzie, can I get a lift?" Tobi asks. She sees my expression change to desperation. "I'm sorry, Em! But I need a ride home tonight and no one else lives near me. I'm sorry I can't stay to help with the clean-up." She is putting on her coat when she remembers something. "Oh, I forgot to tell you that Jeremy was here. He and B.B. came just for a little while, right after you left."

I don't even care at this point. I am too busy pulling the last partier off the couch and pushing him out the door. Ozzie and Tobi are the last to leave and I close the door behind them. I look around the condo in absolute horror. The place is a disaster – food crumbs all over the furniture, half empty cans and bottles, a chair on its side. It'll take me forever to get everything back to normal. Thank God my mother has only been dropping in on weekdays.

Maddy tackles the kitchen and I start cleaning the living room, picking up cushions and pulling chairs back into their spots. I grab a big garbage bag and toss bottles, cans, and paper plates into it haphazardly.

"You'd better check the bedroom too," Maddy suggests when I come into the kitchen for a dishcloth. "I saw Donnie and Kelly coming out of there."

"Seriously?" I go down the hall and open Grams' door to see what shape the room is in. The blankets are rumpled so I smooth them a bit, thinking how my mother would totally lose it if she knew that someone had been in this room. Looking around, I can see that I'm going to have to clean in here too, but then I get an uncomfortable feeling that something is wrong. Something is different.

My stomach sinks as I realize what has happened. Things are missing: the gold thimble from Grams' dresser. A framed gold coin. I scan the room in a panic, trying to remember what else she had kept in there. Her pictures are still in place, her television is on the dresser, and her jewelry box is still beside it. The jewelry box! I consider it for a moment, then step toward it nervously, open the lid, and look inside.

Oh my God. We've been robbed!

I am *so* dead.

Chapter 12

I drop to the side of the bed, the jewelry box in my hands. I've invited thieves into my Grams' home. They've stolen her things – her memories. Diamond earrings that my grandfather had bought for her. Gold bracelets from Spain and Morocco. Silver from Mexico. Every piece had meaning to her.

I have to *fix* this somehow. I have to make it better.

"You have to call the police," Maddy tells me when I finally go into the kitchen and tell her.

"I can't." I grab some paper towels and go back to the bedroom with her in close pursuit.

"You have to or else you'll never find the thief!"

"I can't," I insist as I wipe spilled soda from the top of the dressing table. "I still have time before Grams gets home to figure out who has done this. Maybe I can get everything back."

"You're not a detective, Em." I don't answer. I'm convinced that the stickiness will never wash off this table. "What are you doing? You're not cleaning up, are you?" she asks in horror, grabbing my arm. "You have to leave the scene of the crime exactly the way it was."

"Too late," I say, shaking her off and leaving the room to look for some spray cleaner. She follows me, aghast at what I am doing.

"Well then, I'll call them. They should be here, dusting for fingerprints." She's trying to grab the cloth from me, but I hold it high in the air out of her reach. She looks kind of funny trying to jump for it.

"What's the use of fingerprinting at this point? Everyone we know was here and even *my* prints will be everywhere. And besides, we'll *all* be in trouble for being in the condo, right? We're probably all guilty of trespassing, or illegal entry or something. I'm surprised one of the neighbors didn't call the police earlier."

She puts her hands on her hips angrily. "You know what, Em? I'm not going to help you cover up a crime. I'm going home." She sounds all holier than thou.

"I'm doing this for all of us," I tell her again, but she doesn't seem to get it.

"Don't bother coming back to my house for the night," she says haughtily, heading out the door.

"I'll probably be *cleaning* all night," I call after her. "Because of *your* party!"

* * *

I expect everyone to be asleep when I get home at almost three in the morning, but my mother is reading in a chair in the living room.

"What are you doing home?" my mother asks with surprise.

Shrugging, I try to sound casual. "Maddy and I had a big fight so I took a cab home. It's no big deal. Why aren't you in bed?"

My mother shakes her head and sighs. "I really don't like the idea of you taking a cab at this hour. You should have called me to come get you. I was up anyway – couldn't sleep. Too much to think about." I nod and she stands to give me a hug. "I was just about to make myself some tea. Do you want some? Or maybe hot milk?" After what I have done, I don't deserve to be treated so nicely right now, and it brings tears to my eyes. My mother must think I'm upset about fighting with Maddy.

"Come on," she says, giving my shoulder a pat. "It'll help you sleep."

"It's okay," I tell her, wiping my eyes and moving away. "I think I'll just go to bed." I can't face the thought of sitting in the kitchen and having to lie about the party to cover up what has really happened. I give her a kiss and feel kind of bad as I leave her there alone. I hope she doesn't stay up all night.

★★★

In the morning, I go downstairs, dreading that Grams will be calling soon for her regular Sunday chat. Even though I'm not at all hungry, I decide to make bacon and eggs for everyone.

Frankie comes into the kitchen wearing only his pajama bottoms, his broken arm held across his chest in a sling, his good hand scratching his head. "What are you doing?" he asks, as he shuffles over to the fridge and gets the juice.

"Making breakfast. What does it look like?"

"Not like anything I've ever seen *you* do

before," he quips.

"Mom looked so tired last night. I just thought I'd do something nice for her … for a change."

"She isn't here," Frankie says, pouring his juice over at the table.

"Oh. Where is she?"

"She told me last night she was going to go to church today," Frankie says.

Church? She must be in really rough shape if she's resorting to that. I whisk up the eggs anyway and pour them into the pan to cook. What if she decides to drop over to Grams' place after the service? I have cleaned as well as I can, and I've put the jewelry box back on her dresser, but what if she notices that something's missing? I tap my foot nervously as I stir the eggs.

When we sit down to eat, I decide to tell Frankie what has happened. He looks surprised, but not as devastated as I am. It wasn't *his* party, so I guess he figures it isn't his problem.

"I bet I know who stole her stuff," Frankie says with his mouth full.

"Who?" I ask urgently.

"Jeremy."

Suddenly the smell of bacon and eggs makes me want to gag. I should have known that Frankie would suggest it, that Frankie would pin this on Jeremy somehow. "You are *so* full of shit!" I yell. "Jeremy wouldn't do something like that!"

"Well, who else would? You invited him, didn't you?"

"Yeah, but Tobi said he was only there for a few minutes."

"But he's been there before, he's seen all her stuff –"

"He just went there with me once, while I was watering the plants," I say defensively.

Frankie snorts and picks up some bacon. "Once, huh?"

"Oh, shut up, Frankie! What do you know anyway?"

"Pretty much everything. It's not like it's a secret you two were hanging out there. Practically the whole school saw him going in and out."

"You knew and you didn't tell Mom and Dad?"

Frankie shrugs and then winces, as if the slight movement hurt his arm. "I don't tell Mom and Dad *everything*."

For just a second, I appreciate what he's saying, but then I remember that he's accusing Jeremy of stealing.

"Well, Jeremy didn't steal from Grams. That isn't who he is," I say.

"But he needs money, right?" Frankie says, as though he knows everything. "So he has a motive."

"Stop trying to sound like you're on one of those cop shows. Needing money doesn't make him a thief, so leave him alone."

"He hangs with drug dealers, Em. Don't be so friggin' blind."

I remember the money I had seen change hands between Jeremy and B.B. I quickly push the thought away again. "He's never done anything like that."

He sneers. "How do you know?"

"I just do! He is not a thief. He's not." *But B.B. might be.*

The phone rings and Frankie glances over at the clock. "Ten o'clock. It'll be Grams calling from Italy."

I picture Grams' empty jewelry box. The phone keeps ringing.

"I can't answer it. I mean, what would I say?"

Frankie looks at me, then down at his plate. He jabs his fork into his eggs.

As the call goes to voicemail, I think again of the two short weeks that I have left to make things right before Grams comes home. I push my plate away, the food barely touched, then head upstairs to call Jeremy. I'll need to meet with him to tell him what has happened.

I think of my mother at church and hope that she's putting in a good word for me.

Chapter 13

"So, did you tell your parents or not?" Maddy asks when I catch up to her on the way to school on Monday. I shake my head. "Oh, come on, Em! You probably did a great job cleaning the place and putting everything back together, but your family will know that stuff was stolen when your Grams gets back."

"Not if I can get all the stuff back. I have to figure out who took it and I have to do it fast."

"How?" Maddy asks challengingly.

"On *CSI* they solve crimes in no time at all."

"I know, but they have all that fancy equipment and those labs. This is *real* life. Remember when my mother had her car broken into last year? Even the police couldn't figure out who did that."

"If I don't get everything back, I'll have to replace it."

"How?" she asks again.

"I don't know, but I really screwed up. Grams will never forgive me."

"She's your Grams. She's going to understand," Maddy says kindly.

A few blocks later, Tobi is waiting for us. She doesn't usually walk with us because we're out of her way, so I know that Maddy must have told her what happened. "Are you grounded forever?" she asks me as she joins us.

"My parents don't know anything yet. And they aren't going to, either."

"Right, sure," she says dubiously. "How's Frankie?"

"He'll live. He's not even missing his exams. Mom drove him to school on her way to work."

"What's with that?" Tobi says as she wrinkles her nose. "I'd milk it and say I couldn't write."

"I know, but he's left-handed. Besides, he wanted to go and watch the team finals later. Mom wouldn't let him go there unless he went to school too."

"Your mother is a hard-ass."

"Tell me about it. See why I'm not telling her

anything?" I wonder when my mother will drop in at Grams' this week and whether she'll notice anything different. If I'm lucky, I'll get all of Grams' stuff back before that can happen.

When we get close to the school, I see Jeremy waiting at the entrance, standing with his hands in his pockets as he watches us approach. My heart does a somersault.

"What's *he* doing here?" Tobi asks, scowling over at me.

"I called him and asked him to meet me," I explain, picking up my pace.

"To ask for your stuff back?" she asks pointedly.

"Shut up, Tobi." I cross the parking lot toward him, knowing that Maddy and Tobi are watching us as they walk by slowly. I look and see them stop on the school steps, watching us some more. I wave my hand to tell them to go on. They turn into the school reluctantly.

"How's Frankie's arm?" Jeremy asks.

"It'll be fine. Thanks." I try to find a way to tell him what has happened. "Tobi told me you were at the party and that you brought B.B. with you. Why didn't you stay?"

"You weren't there. And B.B. wasn't into it."

I bite my lip. "There was a robbery at the

party," I blurt out.

"A robbery?" His eyes narrow slightly. "And what, do you think it was me?"

I am taken aback by his bluntness. "No! Of course I don't. Why would you say that?"

He shrugs. "It's what everyone thinks, isn't it? I'm not blind – I saw the looks that Maddy and Tobi were just giving me."

"Some people think that, I guess. But not me. I would never believe that." But I *would* believe it of his friends. I have to ask him, even if it means that Jeremy might never speak to me again. "Jeremy, B.B –"

He cuts me off abruptly. "He didn't do it."

I sigh with frustration. "How can you be so sure?"

"Because I know him."

His belief in B.B. is as strong as my belief in Jeremy. I don't want to press the point, but I'm sure that Jeremy can see in my face that I'm not convinced.

"You don't know everything, you know. Things aren't always the way they seem."

"Okay, fine. But you've got to understand how this looks. I mean, he's got a bad reputation."

"So? Do you think he cares?"

"No. I don't think he cares, but *you* should.

As long as you live in this town and hang with those guys, people will think you're just like them. If the police find out about this robbery …" My voice drops off as he stares at me. I remember how I felt the first time I saw him waiting for Maddy outside the bus, how I had wanted him. I still want him, but I know now that I need to let him go. I step back from him, speaking quietly. "You should move to Albany with Jill."

"My mother is here. She needs me to take care of her."

"She's never even home." I try to keep my eyes from filling.

He kicks at the gravel with the toe of his worn shoe. "Look, I should get to school," he tells me, taking another step back. "I've got my last exam today and I'll fail if I miss it."

★★★

That afternoon, Maddy, Tobi, and I are trying to study in the library, but I can't concentrate. I'm worrying about everything – how I'm going to face Grams when she gets home, whether I'll be able to find her missing jewelry, who could have done such a horrible thing to me and my Grams, and how to prove that it wasn't Jeremy.

"I really need to find the thief," I whisper to them. "It's the key to fixing this entire mess. Besides, it's the only thing I can do to redeem myself. Will you help me?"

The girls agree to help. We push our books aside and put together a list of all the people who were at the party. Tobi tells me to write B.B.'s name down, and Jeremy's, and after a moment's hesitation, I do. When we have all the names, we start at the top and begin making notes. I find myself distrusting everyone. Even people who had always seemed like loyal friends are coming up short as I try to remember what they were doing at the party.

"Jessica *loves* jewelry, and she was in the bedroom," Tobi reminds me.

"Kelly and Donnie were in there forever too. He didn't waste much time getting over Andrea, did he?" Maddy adds.

I hit my forehead with frustration. "We were at the hospital for over three hours. Anybody could have gone into the bedroom in that length of time."

"What do you think about Mick? He was pretty wasted on Saturday night. Maybe he didn't even know what he was doing," Tobi suggests. Maddy looks unsure, but we mark it down anyway.

We start rehashing every potentially suspicious action. Several people had gone outside to smoke. What if they had been taking things out and hiding them in the bushes? Donnie had a coat with huge pockets. Ashley had brought a massive purse.

"Jeremy –" Tobi starts.

"Don't say it," I say quickly, scratching his name off the list. Tobi and Maddy exchange a look, but they don't try to argue with me.

"We have to talk to every single person on this list," I decide.

"Are you kidding?" Tobi says with a frown. "They'll all think you're accusing them of robbery."

"We'll just have to be really careful when we ask them about it. Here." I rip the list into three pieces. "We'll each take a third of the list. Maybe someone will know *some*thing."

They take the lists without much enthusiasm. "When am I supposed to study for my exams?" Tobi complains.

"Just *try* Tobi, please?" She stuffs the list in her pocket and sighs.

For the next two days, we try to get people to remember what they had seen and done that night, but half of them could barely remember that they were even at Grams' condo.

"Well, that was a huge waste of time," Tobi says on Wednesday as we discuss our progress before our last exams.

"Where could we find stolen jewelry?" I think aloud.

"I guess we could try the pawnshops downtown. Maybe someone sold her things there," Tobi suggests.

"Tobi! You are so crazy brilliant!" I tell her excitedly. "We'll go right after school."

"Great, that's exactly how I imagined celebrating the end of exams," she says sarcastically.

I head for class with a new air of confidence.

After school, we meet and head downtown, going first into a musty shop with barred windows. There are two creepy men working behind the counter, both pock-faced with sideburns straight out of the 70s. Their eyes follow us as we check the display cases. I don't see any of Grams' jewelry.

"Sorry it was a dead-end," Maddy says, trying to lift my spirits as we leave the store. "There must be other places though."

We try two other shops, but still nothing. I

completely lose my sense of optimism. In an attempt to cheer me up, Tobi spends ten dollars on a tacky clock with a picture of Paula Abdul on the face. It is time to admit that our investigation is utterly hopeless. Maybe Maddy had been right along. Maybe I should have called the police.

★ ★ ★

When I get home from the pawnshops, Frankie's shoes are on the mat by the door. I kick mine off, and head for the stairs. Maddy, Tobi, and I may have run out of ideas on how to track down the stolen goods, but before I give up completely, I'm hoping that Frankie can come up with another angle. He's all about the angles.

His bedroom door is closed, so I knock and head in without waiting – the way I always do. As I step through the door, he is turning quickly away from me, scooping things up from his bed with one hand and shoving them into his gym bag frantically, trying to hide something. His head then spins toward me, his eyes wide. "I thought you were downtown," he says guiltily. The camera he got for his birthday last year is on the bed.

My eyes fall from his, down to his hand. He's

holding a gold and sapphire bracelet, dropping it into the gym bag as I watch. For the briefest moment, I feel a surge of elation. Grams' bracelet! Frankie has found Grams' things!

But then I see the entire picture – the unzipped gym bag, the rings and pendants lying in a heap inside it, and Frankie's flushed face as he moves to try to block my view. My elation gives way to a dreadful realization.

"Oh shit, Frankie," I moan as I fall to the edge of his bed. "*You* stole from Grams?"

Chapter 14

As a rule, Frankie is rude and insensitive. But this is a whole new level of screw-up that even *I* have never reached, and I don't know how to wrap my head around it. "Why? Why would you do this?" I ask incredulously.

"I needed the money." He drops into his computer chair and rubs his cast absently. "I had a debt I needed to pay and I couldn't get the cash. I didn't know what else to do."

"What? Why didn't you just tell Mom? She would have given you the money."

He shakes his head. "I couldn't. Look, Em, there's some stuff that's been going on for a while, stuff you don't know about. It's not like I *planned* to take anything, but when I was at Grams' I just saw the opportunity. I went into her room when there was no one around, shoved the things into my pockets, and then hid them in the trunk of my car when I went down for Maddy's gift."

I am stunned. "And what about this debt? What's that about?"

He looks up but avoids my eyes. "I've been gambling, okay? Online." He turns and hits a computer key. A poker site appears in bold black and red. "I owed *three grand*."

"Three thousand dollars? Are you insane?" I sit motionless for a minute or more before he answers.

"I was up by a lot," he explains earnestly. "I had won a couple of games, long-shot wins, and I was up. I started losing, but I kept winning a bit back, just enough to keep me going. Then I just got unlucky. I lost a few hundred, then a few hundred more …"

"Oh my God. Mom is going to kill you."

"Mom isn't going to know," he says.

"We have to tell her," I insist.

"Why?" He pats the gym bag. "Look, Em. I've got practically everything still here. We'll return it."

"*Practically* everything? Where's the rest of it?" I demand.

"I sold a couple of things, okay? I was desperate. It was all I could think to do." He leans forward, his forearms on his knees.

I start to feel queasy. "But what if Grams calls the police?"

"What if she does? Why would they think it was me? They'd be more interested in Jeremy. Everyone knows he was there."

"But he didn't do it!" I cry out.

"It's not like it would matter. His life is already so screwed up, it couldn't get any worse."

"But he's not a thief!"

"Three grand, Em! Three grand!" He looks up at me and suddenly his face is crumbling. I watch him break down and cry. I've never seen Frankie cry. Never. I reach across and put my hand on his shoulder, but he pushes me away and turns to look out the bedroom window.

"Can you get back what you sold?" I ask quietly.

He doesn't answer for a moment, then shakes his head. "I doubt it. I sold them online. They've already been mailed out."

I look at the camera on the bed and realize that he had just been taking photos so that he could sell the rest. We'll never see some of Grams' things again and there's no use in trying to cover it up anymore. "Just tell the truth," I implore. He doesn't answer.

I want to shake him for being such a liar. "Frankie, we have to tell the truth."

He is silent for a moment. "Just give me some time, Em, okay? I need to think." His eyes are pleading with me.

"Only until the morning," I finally answer.

***

Later that night, there is a ghostly light shining into the hallway from Frankie's room. It's one thirty in the morning and he's sitting in front of his computer, staring at a sports betting site.

"What are you doing?" I whisper as I slip into his room. I sit at the foot of his bed, tucking my feet up and hugging my knees.

"Nothing."

"You're not gambling again, are you?" I ask worriedly.

"No. Just trying to figure out what to do."

"Me too." I haven't been able to sleep at all. I feel awful for ever having that dumb party in Grams' condo, and I'm completely freaked out about Frankie's situation. I'm not sure that I can remain silent about it for much longer.

His fingers reach out and toy with the keyboard. He finally hits the return key and the site goes into motion.

"Jesus, Frankie! You *are* gambling!"

"Shhhh! I can win it back," he insists, watching as the cards appear on his screen.

I look at him for a moment, then unfold my legs and tiptoe silently out of the room. I've never been a snitch. Frankie and I have shared a lot of secrets over the years, but this time he's in over his head and I don't know how else to help him.

I return a few minutes later with Mom behind me, her pajamas rumpled and her hair askew. Despite the late hour, she is wide awake. And worried.

"What's going on?" she asks, crossing her arms over her chest.

Frankie turns, startled by her voice. He looks shocked, then angry. "Em! I can't believe you!"

I ignore him and turn to my mother. "I did a really stupid thing," I begin, going back over to Frankie's bed and sitting on the edge. "I had this party. Maddy's party. It wasn't at Tobi's, it was at Grams'."

"Emily!" She throws her arms out in disgust. "I give up."

I don't let her reaction get to me. I tell her

about the party – the crowd and the broken vase. "I just want to apologize, because it was a terrible thing for me to have done and I'm really sorry. And I'm going to tell Grams."

Before Mom can respond, I continue. "And there is something else, too." I can hardly get the words out. "When I was cleaning up afterward, I noticed that some of Grams' things were gone."

"Gone?" Her eyes widen. "One of your friends robbed my mother's home?"

I swallow. My heart is pounding.

"No. It wasn't any of her friends," Frankie says quietly, leaning forward in his computer chair. "It was me."

My mother's frown line deepens. "I don't understand … "

"It was me!" he repeats challengingly. He stands and goes to his closet, pulls out the gym bag, and puts it on the foot of the bed. He unzips it angrily, then reaches in and pulls up a handful of valuables. He holds them out toward Mom as though she had demanded to see them and then tosses them back into the bag. His cheeks are blotched, his eyes avoiding hers.

"Wha …" She stops, steps forward, and looks in the bag to be sure of what she has just seen. "Why would you take your grandmother's jewelry?"

Frankie returns to the computer and strikes a key. The black and red screen flashes his last hand. "Because of this," he says. I draw my knees up and grip them with my arms. "It's a gambling site," he clarifies.

"You're *gambling*?" she asks him with a look of dismay. She stands over him at the computer. "How long has this been going on?"

"Almost a year," Frankie mumbles.

"*A year*? You've been gambling online for a year?" She drops onto the foot of the bed beside the gym bag, careful not to touch it. "I need to call your father," she finally says quietly. But she doesn't move.

"How did you pay for this betting? Wouldn't you need a credit card?"

He nods.

"Well?" She keeps staring at him until he answers.

"I got one. From … the mail." My mouth drops open.

"The mail?" My mother's face is gray.

"A card came in the mail one day. It just had to be activated. I called the number and – "

"You've been gambling under *my name*? What about the statements? The monthly statements?"

"I asked for the statements to be sent online so I could delete them," he tells her, his face incredibly red.

She shakes her head in disbelief, walks to the computer, and pushes Frankie out of the chair. He sits next to me on the bed and I touch his good arm for just a second. She sits for ages, scrolling through his screens, looking at the sites he has recently used.

"Poker sites, casino sites, sports betting ..." Her skin looks sickly pale in the half-light. "None of this makes any sense. How could I have missed this?" she asks herself aloud. "How could I not have known what you were doing up here all this time?" She turns and looks at him. "I just don't get it. How did this happen?"

"I started with the free sites," Frankie explains, his eyes lighting up as he rises and moves to the computer, leaning over her to hit a few keys. "They're just like the real sites, but for practice. You can go on and play for nothing, and it's fun, and it doesn't cost anything. They let you win more often though, so they can get you hooked. I'll show you, they –"

"Don't!" my mother snaps as she puts her hands up in the air. She drops to her knees and crawls under the desk. She haphazardly yanks on the wires, unplugging the computer from the wall, disconnecting the mouse, and tugging at the printer cable. If Frankie wants to keep gambling, it won't happen here.

"Counseling," my mother spits as she winds a cable around her hand. "You'll have to go for counseling. And Gamblers Anonymous. Your father and I will go with you." Frankie just stands and stares at her.

"I have a couple of things listed online," he finally says. "I'll need to take them off."

"A couple of things are already sold," I add.

My mother looks at me as if she had forgotten I was still there. "Go to bed, Emily."

I don't try to argue.

I give Frankie a "Please don't hate me" look, and then head down the hall to my own room.

Chapter 15

The next morning, I find Frankie and Mom in his room. "When we're all dressed, we'll go to Grams' place and put these things back where they belong," Mom says to me. "You must have done quite a job of covering up after that party. I was there yesterday and didn't notice a thing."

I realize that she's not complimenting my cleaning skills. I bite my lip and walk away. I'm about to head for the bathroom to have a shower when the doorbell rings. Mom moans as she rises from the bed and goes to the window. "Now what?" Peering down, she recognizes the person at the door and turns to me. "It's Jeremy," she says.

Relieved to have the distraction, I head down the stairs in my pajamas. After the way we ended things on Monday, I wonder if he has come to make up.

"Hi," Jeremy says, looking at me with a half smile. There is a car in the driveway behind him.

"Hi." I smile back.

"I came to tell you that I'm moving to Albany. Jill came last night to pick me up and take me back with her."

"Really? You're moving?"

"Yeah. Staying here was a mistake. The way things are, I'd probably just end up in an even worse situation. I called my aunt and she said she could help me get an apprenticeship in a guitar shop, so I figured it was finally the right time to go." His eyes are on mine and it hits me again – they are *so* blue.

"I'm really happy for you," I tell him, but at the same time, I realize how much I will miss him. "I hope you'll like it there."

"Yeah, it'll be good. I'll be learning how to make handcrafted guitars. The pay isn't much to start, but it's a cool job."

"You'll be great at it." I kiss his cheek, then hug him tightly.

A girl is walking up the steps from the car, holding a small child with round dimpled cheeks and shining curls.

Jeremy steps back to make room for her. "This is my sister, Jill."

"Hi, Emily. Jeremy has told me so much about you," she says, smiling widely. "He hardly ever tells me *any*thing, but he goes on and on about you. He must *really* like you."

"Oh my God, Jill," he objects good-naturedly. "I wouldn't have brought you here if I thought you were going to make me look like a loser."

"You'd better get used to it," she jokes. I like her immediately.

"And this is Glory," Jeremy tells me. "Glory is Jill and B.B.'s daughter."

Of course! It seems so obvious to me now – Jill left town to raise her baby in Albany with her aunt's help. And Glory's round face, her skin tone, and eyes – she looks exactly like B.B.

"Which reminds me, he gave me another hundred dollars from his welfare check, Jill. I'll give it to you later."

The money that had changed hands! I *knew* that it couldn't have been what it looked like. My instincts about Jeremy had been right all along.

"Straight to her college fund," Jill says smiling. Glory grins widely and struggles to get down. Jill shifts her to the other hip and kisses her cheek.

"Hi, Jeremy," my mother says from behind me.

"Hi, Mrs. Talifer," he answers warmly. "This is my sister, Jill, and her daughter, Glory."

"Hello, Jill. It's nice to meet you. And look at you, little one. What a sweetheart!" my mother says as she tickles the little girl. "Are you going to come in?" I know my mother is exhausted and would probably like nothing better than to go back to bed, yet she is inviting them in as though having company would be a treat.

"Thanks for the offer, Mrs. Talifer, but we can't stay," Jeremy says apologetically. "My aunt and uncle are waiting for us. I'm moving to Albany and I just wanted to say goodbye."

"Well, I'm sure that Em is going to miss you," my mother says, putting her arm around my shoulders and giving me a squeeze. "Maybe you can come visit us sometime."

"I'd like that," he says, but I don't really expect he will ever be back. It's weird: I already miss him, but in some ways, I'm relieved to be saying goodbye. I just don't think I was prepared to deal with Jeremy's issues.

They walk to the old Grand Am, strap Glory into a baby seat, and then climb in. My mother pats my shoulder as we watch them drive away.

The horn honks twice, and then he's gone. Mom and I talk for a while longer, then turn back into the house. "I'm really sorry I threw that party at Grams' place," I tell her.

She nods and tucks my hair behind my ear. "We're going to have to talk about it later. A crowd of kids, probably drinking ..." I know I'm in for a huge lecture after she gets Frankie's mess straightened out.

My mother heads back upstairs, and I go to see Frankie, who is sitting silently in the living room. I fall into the corner of the couch. "Jeremy's gone," I tell him.

"I just couldn't face him," Frankie says, staring straight ahead. "If the police had become involved with this mess, he would have been the prime suspect, and I could have ruined his life ... "

"Yeah." It's tempting to say more, but he's already beating himself up about it. I sit there thinking about all of the mistakes we've made. After several minutes, I go into the kitchen and pick up the phone. Slowly, I dial Grams' cell number. I hope it's not 3:00 a.m. in Italy.

"Emily? Well, this is as good timing as any. I'm already into my second glass of wine."

"Oh," I say nervously. "Um ... Grams, I've got some bad news."

"This seems to be the day for it," she sighs.

"I have to tell you something, Grams. I threw a party at your place last week." There is no response from her end. I take a deep breath and go on. "I should never have done it, and I feel so stupid about it. I didn't have the guts to tell you until now. I'm just so sorry."

The line is quiet for a second. When she answers, her tone is uncommonly solemn. "Frankie called me over an hour ago. He explained everything and apologized."

"He did?" It feels as though a huge weight has just been lifted from my back.

"I don't know what he must have been thinking, getting involved in those gambling sites. They're for fools and bored rich people who don't know what to do with all their money."

"He's going to pay you and Mom back, Grams."

"It isn't the money. It's what those things meant to me."

I am overwhelmed with guilt. "We're both really sorry."

"I know, Emily. He told me that you're the one who helped him to admit what he had done."

I feel a tiny bit of pride in myself for having done the right thing by getting my mom involved, but then I remember that I'm no angel. "We were both idiots."

"Well, if it makes you feel any better, I'm coming up with a suitable punishment for you."

"Oh. Great."

"All right, Emily. I'm going to have to go back into the pool now. There's a young man on the diving board who keeps looking my way."

"Oh, Grams!" I cringe at the thought.

We say our goodbyes and hang up. I'm grateful that she is so understanding and that she still wants to be, well, *friends* with me. I don't know what I would do if I didn't have Grams to call when I need a hug.

My mother comes into the room with Frankie's gym bag. "Hurry up and get dressed," she says. I see Frankie coming from the living room. It's time to put Grams' things back in place and try to make things right again. But I get the feeling that none of us believe that things are ever going to be the same.

Chapter 16

Tobi, Maddy, and I go to a matinee and then decide to go for an early supper at the Thai restaurant around the corner. It's drizzling as we walk the short distance between the two buildings.

"I have a date this Friday," Maddy says casually.

"With who?" we both ask in unison. Maddy hasn't been out in a month – not since Frankie confessed everything and she told him she wanted to just be friends.

"Ryan Hawkins. He goes to Lakeshore."

"Lakeshore *College*?" I ask with wonder.

"Of course, the college. He just finished his first year of the accounting program." She throws it out as if it's no big deal, but we all know that it's a really big deal. Even though we're strict about the older-guy rule, none of us have ever even considered the possibility of going out with a college guy.

"What is he?" I ask. "Eighteen?"

"Almost nineteen," she confides. "But my parents haven't met him yet, so keep it to yourselves. My mother would freak."

"I'm not keeping any secrets, not anymore," I warn her. "My mother and I have been getting along really well lately. Besides, your mother is cool. She'd never lose it the way my mother does."

"Are you kidding?" she asks incredulously. "Your mother is the greatest. Mine is all over me for every little thing. My room is a mess, I never help out around the house, I sleep in too late, I don't do well enough at school …"

"Yeah, but she's *right* about all that stuff," Tobi jokes as we reach the restaurant.

"I know, but do I need to hear it all the time?" Maddy moans.

"At least you never got a tattoo or dated a guy with friends in 'low' places," I joke.

"Oh no, I just went out with Frankie!" Maddy laughs and then realizes that I may be offended. "I'm sorry, Em."

"It's okay," I assure her.

"I didn't mean it. Frankie and I are still good friends," she rushes to say.

"Really, it's okay," I repeat. "We still can't quite believe what he did. But it's done and over. He made a mistake and he's paying for it." We take off our rain jackets and hang them over the backs of our chairs as we settle down at a small table in the center of the room. "He hasn't been betting at all."

"But how can you really be sure?" Tobi asks gently. "I mean, he could be doing it at someone else's house, or buying lottery tickets, or joining football pools, or anything. He's got an addiction."

"Yeah, I know, Tobi. I know." Even though Mom and Dad have been attending meetings with him, I wonder if he's still at it. While there's no way to be sure, I just have to have faith that he's got the resolve to quit.

Eager to change the subject, Maddy takes a menu from the stand in the middle of the table. "Are you guys going to that concert together this weekend?"

"You make it sound like we're a couple," I quip. "The last time Tobi asked me out, she wouldn't buy me dinner."

"Listen, you're not exactly a cheap date," she

answers. "What about Frankie? Is he going?"

I shake my head. "He doesn't have time. Grams asked him to volunteer twice a week at a youth center. She figures it'll do him good to tell other kids not to get caught up in gambling. Other than that, he just has work. He's trying to earn as much as he can so he can pay Mom back for the credit card debt. His whole paycheck goes to her every week. She's got him on a strict allowance."

"He must hate that," Maddy notes. She runs her finger around the rim of her water glass. "He still owes me money too."

"What?" I ask with dismay. She nods and takes a drink.

"He'll pay you back," I promise her.

"I know. He already swore he would."

"I think he's really ashamed of what he did," I continue. "He's sure everyone is looking at him differently. He's going for counseling for the gambling, but I think they're talking about other stuff too. Mom and Dad go with him sometimes."

"Well, at least you're not the problem child anymore, Em!" Tobi says brightly. "How's your punishment going?"

"I still have to clean Grams' place once a week for two more months. She's pretty good about it though. She told me she had done some really stupid things when she was young too. Oh, and I bought her all new plants, since everything was totally over-watered and they all died. It cost me a fortune."

"Well I'm not buying your supper," Tobi warns.

"What are you going to order?" Maddy asks us.

"I'm ordering French fries." Tobi drops her menu back into the stand.

"It's a Thai restaurant," I remind her.

"Yeah? So? When we're done eating, who wants to go with me to that tattoo place where Em got her dragon?"

"Really?" Maddy asks with a look of disapproval. "Are you going to get one?"

"I'm going to look at the designs and see. Maybe a bumblebee."

"Where? Shoulder? Ankle?"

"I'm thinking right *here*." Tobi pats her rear end playfully.

"Be careful," I warn. "My tattoo got infected."

"You never said anything," Tobi tells me accusingly.

"Because I didn't want to admit my mother was right. I just covered it with gauze and kept putting antiseptic on it. Thank God all of my blood work came back negative. But I still love my dragon! All I can say is just be careful about it." I rub my tattoo proudly.

"See?" Tobi tells Maddy.

"Anyway, I'm done with getting tattoos," I tell them.

"Good for you," Maddy says with relief. "I knew you'd come to your senses."

"I'm getting my navel pierced instead," I grin.

Searching for suspense, action, and mystery?

Fakie
by Tony Varrato
ISBN: 978-1-897073-79-7

At first glance, Alex Miller seems like a typical teen – look closer, and you'll see that his life is anything but normal. Since witnessing a murder, the Witness Relocation Program has changed the identities of Alex and his mother repeatedly, and they need to keep running to stay one step ahead of his enemies. His latest identity as a skateboarder in Virginia Beach is no easy ride – he'll have to fake it to stay alive.

written by Tony Varrato
Lobster Press™

CD-Ring
by William T. Hathaway
ISBN: 978-1-897073-29-2

Looking for fast cash to buy back his band's repossessed gear, Gabriel gets sucked into a media piracy ring.

"...outstanding ... **CD-Ring** will draw you in from the first page and hold you captive until the last ... bold and thought provoking storyline, with a knock-out conclusion, this work has it all." – *Midwest Book Review*

"Hathaway cooks up a novel that leaves the reader on the edge of their seat ... would make an awesome blockbuster movie." – *teensreadtoo.com*

www.lobsterpress.com • myspace.com/lobsterpress